One supposed prom date, coming right up . . .

"For your information," I told Madison and Rose, aka Snob Central, "I *am* going to the prom. And I'm wearing *this* dress."

Rose snorted. "Who's your date? Your cousin? Or maybe an older brother?"

Madison snickered, and I bit my lip, trying in vain to ignore the painful knot forming in my stomach. I had opened my enormous mouth, and now I was about to pay for it. I looked wildly around the dress shop, searching my brain for the name of a guy—any guy. And then my gaze landed on *him*. Mr. Made-to-be-Naomi-Campbell's-dream-guy.

"He's right over there," I said, pointing toward the total stranger. "He stopped by to check out my dress."

Rose's eyebrows shot up into her bangs, and Madison seemed on the verge of drooling.

"Bye!" I shouted across the store to him. "See you later!"

Why did I just do that? I asked myself. As if I hadn't dug myself into a deep enough hole by announcing this guy was my prom date . . . now I was giving him the chance to unwittingly cause the most humiliating moment of my life.

Prom Trilogy

Justin & Nicole

ELIZABETH CRAFT

BANTAM BOOKS
NEW YORK · TORONTO · LONDON · SYDNEY · AUCKLAND

RL: 6, AGES 012 AND UP

JUSTIN & NICOLE

A Bantam Book / March 2000

Cover photography by Michael Segal.

Produced by 17th Street Productions, Inc.
33 West 17th Street
New York, NY 10011.

ISBN: 0-553-49319-1

Visit us on the Web! www.randomhouse.com/teens

Published simultaneously in the United States and Canada

Bantam Books is an imprint of Random House Children's Books, a
division of Random House, Inc. BANTAM BOOKS and the rooster
colophon are registered trademarks of Random House, Inc. Bantam Books,
1540 Broadway, New York, New York 10036.

PRINTED IN THE UNITED STATES OF AMERICA

OPM   0 9 8 7 6 5 4 3 2 1

One

Nicole

I WASN'T THE kind of girl who rushed home to read her horoscope in the back of *Seventeen* every month. I didn't care whether or not all astrological signs indicated that I would fall in love sometime during the thirty-one days of May. And I never daydreamed about guys on horses sweeping me off my feet or stared at engagement rings in jewelry-store windows.

I, Nicole Gilmore, have never been accused of being a romantic. During my seventeen years on the planet, I have never carved a boy's initials in a tree or doodled his name on my notebook.

But there was something about the floor-length, lavender silk dress that hung in the window of Claire's Boutique that took my breath away. I had been working after school and on weekends at

Claire's for several months now, and during every shift I expected someone to come in and purchase that dress for the upcoming senior prom. So far, the dress was still on the mannequin, and the prom was less than a week away.

Not that the senior prom was relevant in *my* life. I didn't have a date, and I didn't want one. None of the guys at Union High had fallen prey to my particular brand of charm. Consequently I would be staying home on prom night, watching reruns of *Saturday Night Live* and eating cookie dough.

I had told my two best friends, Jane Smith and Christy Redmond, over and over again that I didn't care about the stupid dance. But in those rare moments when I peered deep into my soul, I had to admit, at least to myself, that the prom fantasy held some pretty powerful images.

Even I could appreciate the attraction of a gorgeous date, a beautiful corsage, and a romantic slow dance with the guy of my dreams. But it was just that—a dream. Because there was no gorgeous date. There was no date, period. So why make myself feel bad?

I pushed all thoughts of the prom out of my mind and turned to the inventory list that my boss, Claire, had asked me to compile. *Boring,* I thought, but I tried to concentrate. Anything to keep me from stealing stares at the dress. *My* dress.

The bell over the door of the shop chimed, and I glanced up to see Christy and Jane entering.

"Hey, guys!" I called. "I thought you'd never get

here." I had been looking forward to seeing my friends all afternoon.

"Are you kidding?" Jane asked. "I have been *dying* to try on my new and improved prom dress."

"Me too," Christy agreed. "I want to make sure that Claire cut off enough from the bottom so that I won't be tripping over my own feet the whole night."

I walked over to a rack behind the cash register and pulled off two plastic-covered dresses. "Don't worry. They're perfect," I assured the girls. "Since you two are my best friends, Claire promised she was going to do her absolute best on these dresses—she says her tailoring is like performance art."

Jane took her dress from my outstretched hand. "When Max sees me in this, he's going to forget that any other girl exists."

I politely resisted the urge to roll my eyes. Ever since Jane and Max had realized a week ago that they were madly in love, Jane had talked about little else. Who could blame her? Max was a best friend, a gorgeous guy, and a prom date—all rolled into one. Jane deserved to be happy—even if happiness meant that she was now limited to one topic of conversation: Max Ziff.

"I wish I were as excited about the prom as you are, Jane," Christy commented.

I felt a wave of sympathy for Christy. Her mom had been sick for a long time, and the main reason Christy wanted to go to the prom was to fulfill her mother's longtime wish to see Christy in a long taffeta dress with a corsage pinned to her waist.

"I'm in la-la land again, aren't I?" Jane asked, wincing.

Christy and I laughed, nodding in an exaggerated way.

"Okay, okay," Jane said, her blue eyes sparkling. "But you know, Nicole, I still think you should ask Leon Strickler to the prom. The dance isn't going to be the same if you're not there with us."

"No way," I answered quickly. "I'm not going to a dance with a guy who would rather dissect a frog than kiss a girl good night." I paused. "If I can't do the prom right, I don't want to do it at all."

Almost involuntarily my eyes wandered back to the lavender dress. I had meant what I said—I wasn't about to beg my biology-lab partner to accompany me to the prom just so I could show my face in the gaudily decorated gym on a Saturday night. I had way too much pride for such a desperate measure. But there was no doubt that I wished I could wear that dress.

"Nicole, you've been mooning over that dress in the window every single time I've been in here," Christy said. "Why don't you try it on?"

I shook my head. "No way."

Jane raised one eyebrow. "Come on. Isn't there a tiny little part of you that wants to put on a beautiful dress and join the rest of teenage America in this grand rite of passage?"

I snorted. "No offense, but you're both attaching *way* too much importance to the prom. I mean,

4

what's the big deal? People come, they drink punch, they dance badly, and then they go home."

"There's a *bit* more to it than that," Christy insisted.

"Oh, right. I forgot the part about how all the couples get a cheesy picture taken of themselves standing under some trellis covered with fake roses. Then they tack the photo to the bulletin board hanging over their desk for the next twenty-five years." I was really getting into my speech. "Face it—the whole ritual is idiotic. Especially considering the paltry selection of guys at Union High!"

Jane had been watching me with a patient expression on her face during my entire diatribe. Now she smiled in a Mona Lisa kind of way. "If you *really* don't care about going to the prom, then why is trying on one little dress such a production?" she asked. "Why don't you just humor Christy and me?"

I sighed. Once those girls had an idea in their heads, there was no way to convince them to let it go. I glanced at my watch. My shift was officially over in one minute . . . and I really *did* want to try on the dress. Just for fun. It wasn't as if seeing that beautiful piece of material on my body would do any *harm*.

"Fine! I'll do it." I walked over to the store window and unzipped the dress. Then I slipped it over the mannequin's head.

"I hope she doesn't get arrested for indecent exposure!" Jane commented, pointing at the now naked mannequin.

I laughed and covered the mannequin with a beautiful pink dress. "Can you guys keep an eye on the register? Claire should be back any second."

"No problem," Christy answered. Twice during visits to the shop, Christy had been asked by Claire to watch the register while we dashed in the back to fix an irate customer's dress. "Maybe if I make a sale, Claire will give me a discount on my dress."

"Don't count on it!" I called as I stepped into one of the boutique's three dressing rooms.

I pulled the curtain shut, then kicked off my penny loafers and slipped out of my black pants and white button-down blouse. Inexplicably, my heart was beating wildly in my chest as I pulled the prom dress over my head.

Reaching back, I pulled up the long zipper of the dress and clasped the tiny hook at the neck. I took a deep breath and turned to view myself in the three-way mirror.

"Wow!" I exclaimed. I looked, in a word, amazing.

The pale lavender silk contrasted beautifully with my dark, mahogany skin. The sleeveless cut of the dress set off my long, slender arms and pronounced collarbone. I looked like a prom queen in this getup!

Who am I kidding? I asked myself, sighing. I hadn't had a decent date since the middle of my freshman year, and there were zero prospects on the horizon. I needed this dress about as much as I needed an extra arm attached to my body. There was simply no way that I was going to score a date to the senior prom. And that was that.

It's not like some totally gorgeous guy is going to walk up to me out of the blue and ask me to the prom, I reminded myself. As if! All right, all right. I *did* care that I wasn't going to the dance. And because I cared, I had no desire to dwell on the hopeless situation.

I couldn't wait to get this stupid dress off my body. I was ready to transform back into my usual nonromantic self, who didn't care about stuff like corsages and slow dancing.

"Get out here, Nicole!" Christy ordered from outside the dressing room. "We want to see you in that awesome dress!"

"Too late! I've already changed back into my clothes!" I called—an outright lie. Why have Christy and Jane ooh and ah over how great I looked for absolutely no reason?

"We don't believe you," Jane practically shouted. "And if you don't come out, then we're coming in."

"Yeah," Christy agreed. "We didn't badger you into trying on the dress just so you could hide in the dressing room."

Again I sighed. I never should have caved about trying the dress on in the first place. But since I *had,* I knew that those two wouldn't shut up until they had seen me with their own four eyes.

"Okay, okay. You guys win." I opened the curtain and walked out into the boutique.

"Hello!" Christy yelled. "Can you say 'cover girl'?"

Jane was beaming, the way people in love are constantly beaming and casting loving glances at anyone in a five-mile radius. "Nicole, you look absolutely amazing. Beautiful!"

Christy and Jane's praise made me feel suddenly shy. "Yeah, well, I guess I clean up okay," I murmured. "I mean, who wouldn't look decent in a dress this pretty?"

"Me, for one," Christy commented. "And a lot of other people too."

I strutted back and forth in front of the mirror, admiring myself. I pivoted, then found myself staring into the biggest pair of chocolate brown eyes I had ever seen. Suddenly I teetered in my high heels.

The guy standing in front of me was one of the hottest male specimens I had ever laid eyes on. He was over six feet tall, with dark, smooth skin, and close-cut hair. The rest of the face and body definitely did justice to that amazing pair of eyes.

"Excuse me . . . ," he murmured tentatively.

My heart pounded. Could this be the mysterious stranger I had been fantasizing about just a moment ago? *Will you allow me the honor of accompanying you to your senior prom?* I mentally finished for him.

"Yes?" I responded, flashing him my most dazzling smile.

"Does, uh, anyone know if this place has a juniors' section?" he finished.

I blinked. And then I saw that my Mr. Wonderful was standing in front of a little girl. Well, not so little. Maybe eleven or twelve. Since he was about my age, she must be his sister.

My face suddenly felt like it was on fire. "Uh, not—not really," I stammered. "Try a store called Girl Kraze. It's on the first floor of the mall."

"Thanks." He turned to the girl and nodded toward the door of the store. Unfortunately she waylaid him at the basket of rhinestone barrettes. Great! There was no doubt I was going to feel stupid for my involuntary daydream until Beautiful Boy exited Claire's Boutique.

"I've got to get out of this thing," I informed Jane and Christy. "Claire's not back yet. And we could have customers anytime."

"Speaking of customers, look who's heading this way," Jane said, her eyebrows raised.

I rolled my eyes as Madison Embry and Rose McNeal flounced into the shop. They were two of the most popular—and meanest—girls at Union High. A couple of weeks ago their best friend, the Queen Mean, Shana Stevens, had conspired with Madison and Rose to humiliate Jane in front of half of the senior class. Luckily Jane had come out of the situation with no visible scars (plus one cute boyfriend).

Since then I had made it my personal mission to let the girls know exactly how I felt about them. They hadn't seemed too thrilled when I announced in the crowded cafeteria one day that a pet rock had a better personality than their entire clique put together.

Now Rose stopped right in front of me. Slowly she studied me from head to toe, then gave me a look somewhere between a sneer and a frown.

"Can we get some *help?*" Rose asked, her voice dripping with snotty attitude. "Some of us actually *have* prom dates—and *need* a dress."

I felt like I had been punched in the stomach. This afternoon wasn't going well. And I had a sense that it was about to get worse.

TWO

Nicole

WHITE-HOT ANGER FLOWED through my veins as I stared at Rose and Madison. Maybe I wasn't an airheaded cheerleader, but I wasn't exactly wallflower material either. And the Snob Patrol had no right to speak to me as if I were some scared, dorky freshman. Who did they think they were?

I gave them an acid smile. "For your information, I *am* going to the prom. And I'm wearing *this* dress."

Out of the corner of my eye I saw Christy and Jane glance at each other. But they kept their mouths shut—luckily.

Rose snorted. "Who's your date? Your cousin? Or maybe an older brother?"

Madison snickered, and I bit my lip, trying in

vain to ignore the painful knot forming in my stomach. I had opened my enormous mouth, and now I was about to pay for it. I looked wildly around the large shop, searching my brain for the name of a guy—any guy.

And then my gaze landed on *him*. Mr. Made-to-be-Naomi-Campbell's-dream-guy. Actually, I was staring at his back. He and his sister were headed out the door. But even from behind, he was beautiful.

"If you must know, my date is right over there," I said, pointing toward the mystery man. "He stopped by to check out my dress."

Rose's eyebrows shot up into her bangs, and Madison seemed on the verge of drooling.

"Bye!" I shouted across the store. "See you later!"

Why did I just do that? I asked myself. As if I hadn't dug myself into a deep enough hole by announcing this guy was my prom date . . . now I was giving him the chance to unwittingly cause the most humiliating moment of my life.

The guy turned around. He looked confused—understandably. *Please don't expose me,* I silently begged.

"Uh—bye." He gave me a half wave and sauntered out of the store.

I breathed a huge sigh of relief. I wasn't going to be humiliated—at least, not yet. I turned back to Rose and Madison. "Is there anything else?" I asked, my voice dripping sugar.

I was afraid that Madison was going to chase down my so-called prom date and ask if I were telling the truth. Instead she simply shook her head and returned my fake smile.

"There's nothing here I like. So I guess we'll see you two on prom night," she said. "If he's really your date, that is."

I was doomed. "I can't wait."

With a quick sneer in Jane and Christy's direction, Madison and Rose flounced out of Claire's Boutique. As soon as they were gone, I flopped into a chair next to the dressing rooms.

"What have I done?" I groaned, staring dolefully into the sympathetic eyes of Jane and Christy. "Just put a gun to my head and shoot me now."

"It's not that bad," Christy said encouragingly. "They probably won't even remember this conversation by prom night."

"Right!" As if Rose and Madison *wouldn't* be counting the minutes until they had the chance to rub my face in my lie.

"We'll think of something," Jane promised. "Don't worry, Nicole."

I closed my eyes and sighed. If only I hadn't tried on this stupid prom dress. In the space of ten minutes my once peaceful life had been turned upside down.

Nicole's Journal

(Note to self: This would be good for an essay on the trouble with guys. Like we'd ever be assigned that. I think it's pretty important stuff to examine, though.)

Where do I begin? I mean, I like guys. I don't think they're evil or worthless or generally inferior to the female half of the species. Hey, my dad is a man, and he's a great guy. Most of the time anyway. But at least when they're young, guys have a tendency to act like complete fools. And here's how . . .

First of all, there are *way* too many guys in this world who think that being good at sports means they rule the planet. They believe that their letterman's jacket is, like, an aphrodisiac. I'm sorry, but watching a bunch of boys run around on a football field, hitting one another as hard as they can, doesn't get me in the mood for a romantic walk in the park.

Then there's the other category of teenage male. These are the ones (the science dudes, the valedictorians, the school-newspaper reporters) who nurture their brains plenty—but don't worry about developing an actual personality. They spend all of middle school playing elaborate cyber–video games in their bedrooms, then think they're going to charm girls by expounding on Doom or demonstrating their ability to solve a difficult physics problem.

Here's what I want to know. Where are the guys who like to *talk?* I'm looking to have actual conversations, about actual things. And I'd like to be able to joke around with my dates, the way I do with my friends.

I want a guy to look into my eyes and see *me* for *me.* I want him to care more about that than my chest and cheekbones. And I want to care about him for who *he* is.

Is that too much to ask?

Three

Justin

"CAN I GET shoes to go with my new dress, Justin?" my sister, Star, asked for the tenth time since we had arrived at the mall.

I was staring at a huge, plastic-encased map of the shopping center, searching for the location of Girl Kraze. "We'll see," I said, also for the tenth time. "It depends."

"And I need something for my hair," Star added. "Like a headband. Or some barrettes."

I nodded absently. "This way." I took off in the direction of the store, praying that this would be our last stop.

I had never realized how much effort it took to get a sixth-grade girl ready to go to her first dance. We had been all over two malls, and Star still hadn't found the "right" dress. I was beginning to think that she'd have to wear jeans and a T-shirt to the big event. It was either that or find an outfit that had Star Banks written across the front of it.

But Star's dire need for the perfect outfit wasn't the only thing on my mind. I couldn't stop thinking about that group of girls I had seen in Claire's Boutique. There had been something about them . . . well, *one* of them. But what?

"I think that girl in the fancy dress shop liked you!" Star exclaimed, breaking into my thoughts. "She was, like, totally staring at you."

I rolled my eyes. The moment Star had hit sixth grade, she had begun to talk nonstop about boys—and girls and boys. My little sister saw her eleven-year-old version of romance behind every corner—or dress rack, in this case.

If only Mom were still here, I thought, as I did a thousand times a day. She would have known how to talk to Star about this kind of stuff. I was clueless.

"Nobody was staring at me," I informed my sister. "And you should be more worried about the spelling test you have tomorrow than who *is* or *isn't* looking at who."

"Well, excuuusssse me!" Star retorted. She flipped her long hair over one shoulder and glared at me.

I laughed. Star had a habit of getting on my nerves, but the girl was funny. And I *had* been thinking about those girls from Claire's Boutique. *There was something about one of them . . . ,* I thought yet again.

18

Not that I was interested in anything remotely romantic with *anyone*. I had learned that lesson the hard way. *Don't go there,* I told myself. What had happened last year was old news. The important thing was that I knew what I wanted—and what I didn't want.

I had sworn off the opposite sex until I was at least thirty. Right now I had my hands full taking care of my little sister. And that was all the headache I needed!

"Spell *extracurricular,*" Dad told Star, glancing at the list of words for her spelling test.

"E-x-t-r-a . . ." Star's voice trailed off, and she bit her lip in concentration.

Dad, Star, and I had finished dinner half an hour ago. Now we were all lounging in various areas of the living room, and Dad was quizzing Star for her test tomorrow. This was our tiny family's nightly ritual—our way of keeping things at least seminor-mal now that we didn't have Mom around to make our house a home.

I turned back to *The Grapes of Wrath,* by John Steinbeck, the novel I was reading for my senior English class. I was totally into the book, but my eyelids kept drooping sleepily. All of my years play-ing various sports hadn't prepared me for the amount of energy it took to spend an afternoon shopping with a preadolescent girl.

". . . *c-u-r-r-i-c-u-l-a-r!*" Star finished tri-umphantly.

My dad beamed at her. "Excellent, sweetheart," he exclaimed. "Now all you have to do is spell *archeology,* and you're done for the night."

I put down my book and waited expectantly for Star to spell the word correctly. Before last year I hadn't been the type of older brother who worried about his little sister's quizzes or knew the names of all of her friends. But now . . . well, everything had changed.

" . . . *o-g-y.*" Star's voice interrupted my thoughts. *"Archeology!"*

"Exactly right," Dad announced. "You get an A."

Star grinned. "Can I go call Alison now?"

"Yes, you may." Dad put down the spelling list as Star sprinted from the living room. He turned to me. "Who is Alison?"

"Star's new best friend of the week," I explained. "They bonded during a field trip to the museum."

Dad sighed in this sort of wistful way that always made me feel sad. "Star really is growing up fast, isn't she?"

I nodded. "Sometimes when I overhear her talking to her friends, she sounds like she's older than *I* am."

Dad took off his reading glasses and slipped them into his shirt pocket. "I guess there's nothing we can do about it—you can't stop nature."

"Nope." I wished there was something I could say to my father to make him feel better. But I knew that it was at times like this that he missed Mom most. We all did.

"She would have loved to take Star shopping for

that dress," Dad commented, as if reading my mind. I knew that the "she" he was referring to was my mother. "And she would have loved to see you play in the basketball championship last winter."

"We're doing okay, Dad," I said softly.

And we were. All things considered. It had been over a year since Mom lost her battle with breast cancer. At first Star, Dad, and I had walked around the house like zombies. We had eaten nothing but takeout Chinese food and frozen pizza. The dishes had piled up in the sink, and nobody had bothered to clean the shower. It was dismal.

Then Grandma Banks had come to visit. She reminded us that we couldn't stop living—that was the last thing that Mom would have wanted. And so . . . we had gotten our acts together. For the most part.

My father nodded, and I saw his eyes drift toward a family picture that stood at the center of the mantelpiece. "Before Elaine died, I promised her that I would try to be a mother as well as a father to both of you." He sighed. "But seeing Star changing at the speed of light . . . I don't know if I'm doing such a great job in the mom department."

"Don't worry, Dad," I assured him. "Star is happy. And she's a good kid. She'll be fine."

"And how are you?" he asked me, giving me a penetrating stare. "Are you hanging in there?"

"Sure." I gulped. Talking about my emotions wasn't exactly my forte. I preferred to be the strong-and-silent type.

21

Dad's gaze was so intense that I felt like he was looking straight into my brain. It was a talent that made him the excellent father he was. It was also unnerving.

"You should go out more, Justin. Have some fun." He grinned at me. "I'm sure you would enjoy taking a nice girl to a movie or out to dinner."

"Dad, I'm *fine*," I repeated. "You're doing a great job of taking care of us. Really."

He reached over and gave me a paternal pat on the shoulder. "How about some ice cream?" he offered.

"Sounds good." I turned back to the photograph as Dad retreated into the kitchen.

Looking at the picture now, I still found it difficult to believe that Mom was actually gone. I would never forget the last months of her life. It was as if we were all living through a nightmare. Poor Star. She had been so young, so confused.

I closed my eyes, and images of that terrible time flooded through my memory. I remembered sitting in the waiting room of the hospital with Star, waiting for Dad to come out of Mom's room to tell us how she was doing.

I had known then that Mom's death would be the hardest of all on Star. Her face had been so sad. . . . It had broken my heart into a million pieces.

The waiting room. My eyes popped open, and I snapped my fingers. Now I remembered. I had seen the girl from Claire's Boutique in the waiting room of the hospital. I'd overheard the doctor talking about *her* mother's condition. And it wasn't good.

22

Her mom had cancer too, I recalled. The disease hadn't progressed as far as my own mom's, but the doctors were pursuing a heavy-duty course of chemotherapy. I could still see the girl's tearstained face as she absorbed the news.

I wondered how she was doing—and how her mother was. I hope she didn't have to go through what I experienced last year. *But I'll probably never know,* I thought. Most likely I would never see the girl again.

Justin's Journal

(Note to self: Buy a new notebook—this one's full after this rant about girls.)

I don't *have* any trouble with girls. None. *Nada.* I know better than to *let* girls cause me any trouble. Not that I have anything against them. They're enjoyable to look at, they can be great lab partners, and I've been known to enjoy conversation with a few of them over a disgusting lunch in the Jefferson cafeteria.

But I realized a long time ago that it's dangerous to allow a girl to matter too much to me—unless she's related by blood. I mean, who needs the hassle? I don't want to walk around with my head in the clouds and my heart in the palm of some female's tight grip. I prefer to keep my senses about me at all times.

I guess I need to amend my first statement. I don't have any trouble with girls *now.* I have had trouble in the past—major, major trouble. I fell in love one time, and it's not something I'm looking to repeat. It was one of the worst experiences of my life.

So what was the trouble with *that?* Basically, I trusted a girl with all of my heart. And she took that trust and threw it in my face. Oh, sure, she said she was sorry and gave me the standard it's-not-you-it's-me line. But her eyes were so cold—icy, really—that her mere glance now sends chills down my spine.

I learned the hard way that girls are, in fact, nothing *but* trouble. Unless you keep them at a nice, safe distance where they have no power to inflict any pain whatsoever. Which is why I've decided to devote myself to anything and everything *not* related to females.

Having said all that, I have to admit that I miss hugging and kissing and holding hands. I miss that feeling that I used to get right before my girlfriend answered her front door. Maybe . . . well, maybe that *is* the trouble with girls. I miss them.

Four

Nicole

"**D**O YOU HAVE this in orange?" The mother of a girl in one of the dressing rooms held out a long, black skirt for my inspection.

"Uh . . . no." *Thank goodness,* I added silently. I assumed the daughter wanted to look like a prom queen—not a pumpkin.

I turned back to the stack of receipts next to the cash register. I had made over a dozen sales that afternoon, and each one had required me to make at least a dozen laps around the store, searching for sizes, colors, and matching shoes. I was beat.

And I still had another hour to go. This was already my fourth shift this week at Claire's Boutique, and I was getting behind on my homework. But if I wanted to pay Claire back for that gorgeous lavender prom dress, which she had let me buy on credit, I had no choice but to work double time.

"Do you know where I could *find* this skirt in orange?" the woman called. "Maybe at another store?"

I shook my head. "No, ma'am," I answered sweetly, sounding more like a friendly salesgirl than I felt. "But I think the pink one would look amazing on your daughter."

"Pink?" She brightened. "You know . . . you might be right."

I knew I should walk over to the dress rack and pull out the appropriate garment, but I couldn't seem to make myself abandon my post on the stool in front of the register. *If she can't find the pink skirt herself, I'll offer to help,* I promised myself.

This situation was ridiculous. I was working like crazy to pay for a dress that I was never going to have the chance to wear. As of now, I was no closer to having a prom date than I had been when I announced to Rose and Madison that Mr. Gorgeous was my official date. *Idiot!* I told myself. What had I been *thinking?*

I looked up from the receipts when I heard tinkling from the small silver bell over the door of the boutique. Jane and Christy breezed into the shop and headed toward the cash register. Finally!

"Did you find him?" I demanded, practically pouncing on my two best friends. "Please, tell me you found him." I had sent them deep into the mall with one mission: Find Mr. Beautiful. Once I had him right in front of me, I'd simply ask him to go to my prom with me. If I didn't lose my nerve.

I had been searching for him myself—with zero luck. During every one of my breaks, I roamed the food court, keeping my eyes peeled for a gorgeous guy splitting a basket of french fries with his little sister. I had spotted plenty of cute guys—and a plethora of little sisters—but my mystery man simply hadn't been on the scene since the day I'd first laid eyes on him.

Sending Jane and Christy out to look for him had been my latest attempt to dig myself out of the potentially humiliating situation I faced on prom night. I was hoping that two pairs of fresh eyes would bring me good luck.

Christy shook her head. "Sorry, Nic."

"We searched the place from top to bottom," Jane informed me. "We even went aisle to aisle in, like, fifteen sporting-goods stores. He's not there."

"To tell you the truth, I don't even really know what the guy *looks* like," Christy told me. "I only saw part of the side of his face and the back of his head when we were all in here the other day."

"Well, *I* saw him!" Jane announced. "And I can unequivocally say that I haven't seen him since that day."

I sighed. Things were looking pretty grim. If I didn't show up in my lavender dress at the prom with *that guy,* Rose and Madison were going to have proof that I lied. And I had no doubt that the girls would divulge that fact to anyone and everyone within a mile range.

I have to find him, I thought for the thousandth time. *It's the only answer.*

By ten o'clock that night I was more convinced than ever that the final weeks of my high-school career were about to go up in flames. I had trekked around the mall two more times with no more luck than I'd had before.

Apparently my mystery guy didn't have a habit of cruising malls. I had to accept the possibility— no, the *probability*—that I would never see him again. Much less convince him to take me, a total stranger, to the senior prom.

I stared at the history book sitting in my lap. I had read the same paragraph about the Great Depression three times. And I still had no idea what it said. *Great Depression,* I thought. *Something I should be able to relate to.*

There was a soft knock on my bedroom door, and I gladly looked up from the textbook. "Yes?"

The door opened. My twenty-year-old sister, Gwen, stuck her head through the doorway. "How are you doing, Nic?" she asked. "You barely said a word during dinner."

Gwen's a sophomore at a college a hundred miles away, but she periodically comes home to eat what she calls "real" food and do about a dozen loads of laundry. Usually I loved having my sister back home, but tonight I had been too distracted to grill her about college life.

"I'm having a crisis," I blurted out. "My life is over."

Gwen laughed. "Wow! In that case, it's a good thing I'm here." She walked into my bedroom and shut the door behind her.

I wasn't crazy about the idea of revealing the stupid move I had made with Rose and Madison. Nonetheless, I had a feeling that trying to hide the truth from Gwen was going to be impossible. She had a way of making me tell her everything—even when I didn't want to.

Gwen climbed onto my bed and stuffed a couple of pillows between her back and the wall. She stretched her legs out in front of her and raised her eyebrows at me. "So? What's the story?"

"I don't even know where to begin. . . ." Should I tell her about my showdown with Shana, Rose, and Madison in the lunchroom a few weeks ago? Or should I explain that I hadn't had a date since freshman year because guys had heard I was so picky that there was no way anyone would ask me out?

As Gwen waited for me to spit out whatever it was that I was planning to say, I noticed her eyes drifting toward the open door of my walk-in closet. Her gaze fastened on the floor-length lavender dress that was hanging from a hook on the closet door.

"Hey, is that what I think it is?" she asked.

I nodded. "Yep. A prom dress." My voice was flat.

Gwen grinned. "Who's the lucky guy?"

I could see visions of corsages and boutonnieres dancing in her eyes as she studied the graceful cut of the dress. Gwen, unlike me, had spent every free minute during high school going on dates.

"There *isn't* a lucky guy." I moaned, grabbing a pillow and burying my head in it.

Gwen frowned. "Uh-oh . . . does the dress have something to do with whatever it is that's bothering you?"

I took the pillow away and tossed it across my bedroom. "I'm a complete and total idiot!" I announced to my sister.

She laughed. "I've known you since you were born, Nicole. You might be a little annoying at times, but you're definitely not an idiot."

"You'll change your mind once you hear what I did," I said, sighing deeply.

Gwen leaned forward, preparing to listen intently to my saga. "Well . . . don't keep me in suspense!" she begged. "Tell me what's going on!"

"I told two of the nastiest girls at school that I had a date to the prom," I explained miserably. "But it was a lie."

"Hmmm . . ." Gwen was silent for a moment, gazing at the lavender dress. "So—ask somebody. Anybody."

"I can't ask just *anybody*," I responded, realizing for the millionth time that I had been suffering from temporary insanity when I had told Rose and Madison that Mr. Wonderful was my date.

"Okay . . . I'm missing something." Gwen leaned back against her stack of pillows and looked at me expectantly.

Yeah. You're missing the fact that your sister has the IQ of

32

a termite, I thought. *No, lower than a termite. An amoeba.*

"I told Rose and Madison that I was going to the prom with a certain gorgeous guy. I have to show up with *him,* or I'll be humiliated in front of the entire senior class." I cringed just thinking about the imminent ugly scene with the so-called popular girls.

"You're a beautiful girl," Gwen said in her reassuring-big-sister voice. "I'm sure if you explain the situation to the guy, he would be happy to take you to the prom—as long as he doesn't already have a date."

Of course Gwen thought I was beautiful—she's my sister! But my mystery man was another story. "Well, there's a huge catch—I don't even know the guy's name. He happened to be in Claire's Boutique when Rose and Madison started in on me about not going to the prom . . . and, well, I accidentally pointed to him and announced that he was my date."

"How do you *accidentally* announce that someone is your prom date?" Gwen asked.

I shrugged. "I wasn't thinking. . . . It just sort of popped out of my mouth before I could understand the implications of what I was doing."

"And now you have no idea how to find this mystery dude," Gwen finished, getting the picture.

"Do you think Mom and Dad will let me stay home from school for the rest of the semester?" I asked hopefully. "I could help around the house, or do some work for Dad at his office, or—"

"Not a chance," Gwen interrupted. "I suggested the same thing when I had a series of the grossest zits you've ever seen during the first semester of my junior year in high school."

"Maybe I could alter my appearance, like one of those people in the witness-protection program," I suggested. "You know, wear a wig and sunglasses and a big gauzy scarf around my face."

Gwen reached out and squeezed my hand—a sure sign she was about to give me a well-intended but ultimately useless big-sister lecture. I braced myself for the ineffectual pep talk.

"I know this seems like a really big deal right now, Nic," she began, warming up to her role as the older, wiser one. "But trust me, not having the right date to the prom isn't something that will scar you for life."

"I'm not worried about being scarred for life!" I retorted. "I'm worried about giving Rose and Madison a reason to think they're better than I am!"

Part of me knew that I was being ridiculous. I should have been confident enough not to care what a bunch of jerky girls said about me at school. After high school I would never have to deal with that crowd again.

But still . . . I *did* care. I didn't want to get a copy of my senior yearbook and find myself described as Union High's biggest loser. Sure, I was being shallow. But I had been responsible, and deep, and studious for the last four years. Just once I wanted to be a totally frivolous teenager. I wanted to wear a beautiful dress to the prom—and have an equally beautiful guy on my arm.

And I want to prove to Rose and Madison that I'm not some geek. I'm as attractive and likable—if not more—than any of the girls they hang with. Somehow the prom had become important to me. I simply *had* to go.

"Nic, I really don't believe that your little white lie is going to turn into a life-altering tragedy." Gwen grinned. *"But* if this is really that important to you, then let's go about it the right way."

"The right way?" I squeaked. What was the "right way"? I had already searched for Mr. Adorable numerous times.

Gwen nodded. "You need a plan. A good plan."

I wasn't about to argue with that point. "Go on."

"Here's what you've got to do . . . ," Gwen started.

I grabbed a notebook and pen off my desk, prepared to take notes. I was going to absorb every word Gwen uttered, and then I was going to follow her advice.

Thank goodness for big sisters, I thought. Gwen might be full of lectures. But she was always there when I needed her. *And I definitely need her now!*

Five

Nicole

"**W**HAT ARE YOU *eating?*" Jane asked, warily eyeing the bag of grains I had brought from home for lunch on Monday.

"Power food," I explained. "Gwen says this stuff helps her get her brain in gear when she's got to put in a long night of studying."

Christy wrinkled her nose. "It looks like something I used to feed the horses when I went through my riding-lessons phase."

"This stuff doesn't taste that great," I admitted, biting into another mouthful of the dry, bland mixture. "But if I'm going to find my mystery guy this week, I need all the help I can get."

Jane and Christy exchanged a glance that I mentally characterized as "worried." But neither of them said a word.

" I asked. "Did you find Mr. Beautiful? ave a girlfriend? Did he say he would r consider taking a stranger to the prom, no matter how desperate and pathetic she was?"

Jane set down her taco. "Unfortunately, we *didn't* find him." She shot another glance at Christy. "And to be honest, we don't think we're going to."

"Nicole, we think you might want to forget about this whole thing," Christy added. "I mean, it doesn't look like your dream man is going to show his face again."

"And the prom is *this* Saturday!" Jane chimed in.

"Maybe if you don't say anything else about it, Rose and Madison will lay off." Christy's voice was mild, but her message was clear: *You're doomed.*

I heard what they were saying. I really did. But after my sister-to-sister talk with Gwen last night, I was more committed than ever to finding Mr. X. Still, there was no way I could search on my own. I needed to have my two best friends as resources.

But how could either of them understand what it felt like not to have a date for the prom? Jane was going with Max—of course. And Christy was going with Jake Saunders, who she claimed wasn't her favorite person but was incredibly cute nonetheless.

Just as I was opening my mouth to launch into the details of the plan Gwen had helped me come up with, I noticed two extremely unwelcome individuals heading our way.

"Uh-oh," I muttered. *I think I might be about to say something I'll regret.*

"Hi, Nicole," Rose greeted me. As always, she didn't try to hide the disdain in her voice.

"Hey," I responded casually. "What brings you two to this side of the cafeteria?"

As in all lunchrooms across America, there was an unwritten law at Union High that the cafeteria was divided and subdivided. Students rarely ventured out of the area where they sat every day.

"We were curious . . . ," Madison said. "Has your date come up with an excuse to get out of going to the prom with you yet?"

Yep. Now I was *positive* I was about to say something I would later regret. But there was no way to avoid it. Not unless I was ready to give up the fight.

I fluttered my eyelashes and forced my face into an expression of total serenity. "As a matter of fact, he's completely psyched about the dance," I assured them. "And he decided that the two of us should go to La Serenara before we make our entrance at the prom."

"How interesting," Rose responded, her eyebrows raised. "That happens to be where *we're* going to dinner."

"Then I guess I'll see you there." I couldn't believe how confident I sounded. It was almost as if I actually believed every word that was coming out of my mouth.

As Rose and Madison sashayed toward their side of the cafeteria, Jane scowled. "Those girls get friendlier by the day," she commented wryly. "They bring sunshine to everyone they encounter."

"Uh, Nicole . . . you do realize that you just

dug yourself deeper into this mess, right?" Christy asked, looking concerned.

"Before you two go through the blow by blow about why I should abandon my search for the mystery date, let me tell you about my new plan." I set aside the bag of brain food and leaned forward to deliver the verbal blueprints of my new strategy.

"We're listening," Jane assured me. "But we reserve the right to declare you totally nuts and unable to make your own decisions."

Make this good, Nic, I ordered myself. Without Jane and Christy's help I didn't know if I would have the nerve to conduct an all-out search, my sister's brilliant idea.

"We know he isn't a student at Union High," I said. "And we know he doesn't hang out at the mall all that often."

"I'm with you so far," Christy chimed in. "But you're not telling us anything we don't already know about him."

"*However,* he must go to a high school that's close by," I reasoned. "Otherwise he never would have been at the mall in the first place." Now was the part where I begged them to help me. I took a deep breath. "All *we* have to do is check out the other schools during lunchtime and right after school, and eventually we'll find him—hopefully."

"Nic, there are, like, ten high schools in our vicinity," Jane pointed out. "Do you know how hard it's going to be to find him?"

"And remember . . . I didn't even get a good look

at the guy," Christy reminded me. "I'll be virtually useless when it comes to picking him out of a crowd."

What my friends said made a certain amount of sense. But not enough sense to convince me to abandon my project.

"What if Max was the guy we were trying to find?" I asked Jane. "Would you still believe that looking wasn't at least worth a try?"

"But I *love* Max," Jane answered, her face turning slightly red from embarrassment. "The only reason you want to find this guy is to prove a point. . . . At least, that's what you said."

The truth was that my desire to find Mr. Hottie now went beyond the need to save face in front of Rose and Madison. I *wanted* to go to the prom. And I wanted to go with *him*. There had been something about that guy. . . . I had seen him in my dreams several times over the past few days. I almost felt like I knew him.

"I just know that I won't be able to graduate from high school with a clear conscience unless I at least *try*," I responded, my voice soft and pleading. "Will you guys help?"

Christy grinned. "Of course we will, Nic," she assured me. "We would both do anything for you—you know that."

I breathed a huge sigh of relief. I had the two best friends in the world. And as soon as the three of us found Man with Soulful Eyes, I was going to give them each a huge hug and a big kiss. No, *first* I was going to beg the guy to take me to the prom.

Then I would give them a hug and a kiss.

I just hoped that moment would come to pass. Finding *him* had come to mean everything to me.

"Ms. Gilmore, would you care to respond to the question?" Mr. Schneider's voice interrupted the intense concentration I was directing toward the piece of paper in front of me.

Oops. "Uh, sorry . . . what was the question?" I asked meekly. Usually I was the one raising my hand—not the one doodling in the back row. But it was now Friday afternoon, and how was I supposed to concentrate on anything except for how many hours and minutes I had left to find my so-called prom date?

"Never mind, Nicole. Just try to stay with us for at least the last ten minutes of class." Mr. Schneider gave me a smile, then pointed at Brian Landry, a none-too-bright jock type who was snoozing in the corner of the room. "Mr. Landry, maybe *you* could enlighten us."

I tuned back out as Brian began to stutter unintelligibly. There was simply no chance that I was going to pay even an iota of attention during this U.S. history class. My mind was occupied with far more pressing matters than the Wall Street stock-market crash of 1929.

Like locating my knight in shining blue jeans. Jane, Christy, and I had cruised the parking lots of every high school within a fifteen-minute radius. We had checked out McDonald's, Burger King,

42

Pizza Hut, and a 7-Eleven. And nothing. Not even a glimmer of the guy I had sworn to take to the prom.

Twenty-four hours from now almost every girl in my class would be primping and preening, preparing for their big night. And I would be home alone, counting the minutes until Rose and Madison used the cafeteria as a stage on which to make me eat dirt!

I turned back to the single sheet of paper on my desk. On it I had written a list of every place where I could realistically expect to find my mystery man. Now that all of the original places hadn't panned out, I was trying to come up with more options. *Car wash,* I wrote. But I knew I'd be struck by lightning, sitting at this desk, before I'd find *him* at the exact moment on the exact day at the exact car wash he decided to use.

Desperate, I wrote next, in big, bold capitals. It wasn't a place, but the word definitely suited my frame of mind.

"Nicole?" Mr. Schneider's voice once again broke into my thoughts.

I snapped my head upward and smiled apologetically. "Uh, sorry, what was the question?"

He laughed. "There's no question, Ms. Gilmore. I just wanted to inform you that class is over."

I glanced around the classroom. It was empty, except for a couple of girls who were redoing their lipstick before venturing into the hallway. Man! I had been so into my own head that I hadn't even noticed the loud shrill of the last bell. I was losing it!

"Thanks, Mr. Schneider," I responded sheepishly. "I'll, um, see you on Monday."

I grabbed my backpack from underneath my chair and sprinted toward the door of the classroom. If I stayed in there one more second, I was positive that Mr. Schneider would start grilling me about why I hadn't been paying attention. And a well-meant lecture was the last thing I was in the mood for.

I headed toward my locker, racking my brain for a good spot to search for my mystery man. Unfortunately, my mind was a big, fat blank.

"Maybe I should check out North High again," I said to myself, spinning the combination on my locker.

"Nicole!" Jane appeared at my side and threw an arm around my shoulders. Her face was flushed, and she was grinning as if she had just discovered that chocolate didn't, in fact, have any calories.

"What's up?" I asked. "Did Max tell you he loved you for the hundredth time—or are you just happy to see me?"

"*This* is up!" She pointed to a large, stuffed canvas bag at her feet. "You're not going to believe what I got!"

"What?" I asked. I hadn't seen her this excited since she announced that she and Max were now an official couple.

"I have in the bag last year's yearbooks for every high school in our area!" she practically shouted. "I had a brainstorm during my study hall, paid a visit to the Union High yearbook editor . . . and voilà!"

"I don't get it." I knew Jane was going somewhere with this, but I couldn't quite connect the dots (or the yearbooks, in this case).

"All you have to do is flip through these until you find Mr. Wonderful," she explained. "Once you see his picture, we'll know his name, his school, and all kinds of other vital information."

In a flash it clicked. If I weren't so excited, I probably would have fainted with gratitude. "Jane Smith, you are brilliant!" I yelled.

"We're just lucky that the yearbook editor keeps copies of all of the other schools' books for ideas," she responded.

"Have I told you lately that you're the smartest best friend a girl could ever hope to have?" I gave her a huge hug, then grabbed the first yearbook out of the canvas bag.

"Don't thank me yet," Jane warned. "First we've got to find your guy."

Jane and I knelt down on the semigrungy floor of the corridor. We each opened a yearbook and began to flip through the photos as fast as we could. Page after page of nameless faces passed by me. I began to worry that maybe I *wouldn't* recognize him.

Sure, I had seen him in my dreams (a fact that I alone was aware of), but there was a possibility that I had changed his face in my imagination. Could a mortal man actually be as goodlooking as the guy in my dreams had been?

"Look through this one," Jane advised, handing me the yearbook from Jefferson High. "It feels lucky to me."

I opened the book to the section that pictured last year's class of roughly three hundred juniors. *Adams. Ali. Allen. Alton.* I skimmed through the A's, then started in on the B's. *Babbit. Babson. Bacon. Bailey. Banks—*

"Banks!" I shouted. "Banks!"

"You found him?" Jane slammed the Washington High yearbook shut and leaned over to look at the book in my lap. "Where?"

"Justin Banks," I announced. "Right here." I pointed to the small photograph. Even in a two-by-two picture, the guy was gorgeous. And he looked *exactly* like I had remembered him.

Jane whistled. "He's cute, all right. And that's definitely him." She studied the photo for another few seconds, then frowned. "Nicole, is it really possible that a guy who looks like *that* doesn't have a girlfriend?"

I shrugged. "If he does, I'll just have to buy her off. Because now that I've found Mr. Justin Banks, there's no *way* I'm going to let him turn me down."

"In that case, let's go find Christy," Jane suggested. "If we hurry, we can get over to Jefferson before all of the kids leave—and you're going to need all the moral support you can get."

My heart was pounding as I followed Jane down the hallway toward Christy's locker. Now that I knew Mr. X's name and school, I had only one problem. What was I going to say when I found him?

46

Six

Justin

"JUSTIN, I'M TELLING you, this girl is really pretty," Sam insisted. "You've *got* to go out with her tonight."

I rolled my eyes. My best friend, Sam Patton, had been trying to set me up on dates for the past three months. No matter how many times I said no, he just kept coming at me.

At the moment we were hanging out on the grassy lawn in front of Jefferson High, decompressing after a major chemistry test. Sam was trying to persuade me to double-date with his girlfriend and her cousin, who was visiting for the weekend. On Monday, the first time he'd asked me, I had told him I wasn't interested. He was *still* asking me now that it was Friday afternoon.

"First of all, you have no idea whether or not

Maya's cousin is pretty. You've never even met her." With Sam it was sometimes necessary to point out the obvious.

He grinned. "How could a girl related to Maya *not* be pretty? It's simple genetics, my friend."

"You know I have a rule against dating," I reminded him. "Why would tonight be different from any other night?"

"Justin, I love you like a brother, but this whole I-don't-need-anyone-because-I'm-an-island-unto-myself attitude has got to go." He paused. "Besides, I already promised Maya that we would help her entertain her cousin."

I appreciated the fact that Sam cared about my social life (or lack thereof), but it was also a quality that I found totally irritating. After all, this was *my* life. If I wanted to stay home on Friday night and read a book, well, that was *my* business. And I refused to be guilted into having a so-called good time.

"For the last time the answer is *no*," I announced firmly.

There was no way that Sam was going to change my mind. I wasn't about to open myself up again to the kind of hurt I had experienced last year. That lesson had been learned—and I had no interest in learning it all over again the hard way.

"Justin, you've really got to—" He stopped midplea, and his eyes drifted off to some point over my shoulder.

"What?" I asked, turning around to look.

"Check out those girls!" Sam told me. "They are *hot*—and they're not from Jefferson."

I scanned the parking lot automatically, searching for unfamiliar (but pretty) faces. And then I saw them. Three girls were piling out of a red Honda, and Sam was right. They weren't Jefferson High students.

I frowned. There was something about the girls, though. . . . I felt like I'd seen them before. *If not at school, where?* I wondered, searching my memory.

"Maybe my reputation as the best boyfriend in the world has spread to other high schools, and I'm being pursued by the masses," Sam speculated.

"Yeah, you're a regular Leonardo DiCaprio," I retorted, resisting the urge to snort. Sam was a lot of things—modest wasn't one of them.

"Hey, one of them is heading straight toward us!" Sam said, jabbing me in the side. "Have you been hiding a girlfriend from me?"

I shook my head, studying the girl who was walking toward us. She was tall, with smooth black skin and silky hair. Wearing faded jeans and a white tank top, her well-sculpted arms swung at her sides. *Where have I seen her?* I asked myself again.

I closed my eyes. In my imagination the girl wasn't wearing blue jeans . . . she was in a long, lavender dress. I snapped my fingers. "The mall," I exclaimed.

Yep. That's where I had seen this girl before. Immediately my eyes traveled to one of the other two girls. There she was again. The girl I had recognized from the hospital that day in the dress shop.

Today the girl was smiling, and there were no signs of the tears I had seen streaking down her face in that horrible waiting room. But even from this distance I could see that her grin didn't quite reach her eyes. She had the same sort of distracted air about her that I had had during my own mother's illness.

Her mom's condition hasn't improved, I guessed. As the thought formulated in my brain, my heart went out to her. Unfortunately, I knew exactly how she felt. Just seeing her face, I felt a rush of the grief that had become so familiar during the last year. It was never far from the forefront of my mind.

I was still looking at the girl from the hospital when I realized that the first girl was standing, like, *right* in front of me. I blinked and found myself staring into a pair of huge brown eyes.

"You're Justin Banks," she announced, her hands on her hips.

I glanced at Sam, wondering if he had somehow orchestrated this whole event. But he looked as baffled as I felt. "Uh, yes, I am," I replied. "Do I know you?"

Man. This girl was totally beautiful, and for some strange reason, she seemed to know me. At another time in my life (like, a year ago), I would have thought I was experiencing my own male, teenage version of heaven on earth. But I had trained myself not to care about the way a girl looked—or about anything else that in any way, directly or indirectly, related to the subject of dating.

"You don't know me," she said. "But I have to talk to you."

My mind raced. Had I unknowingly *done* something to this girl? Rear-ended her car in a parking lot? Accidentally knocked over a rack of expensive, breakable merchandise in Claire's Boutique? *There's nothing,* I thought. *I have done nothing wrong.*

"Okay . . . I'm listening." I felt like I was in an episode of *The X-Files* or maybe on *Candid Camera.* A complete stranger (who happened also to be an extremely attractive girl) had appeared out of thin air and demanded to talk to me. Why?

She glanced over at Sam. "Uh . . . *alone?*"

This scenario was getting weirder by the second. I looked over at Sam and shrugged. He backed away, grinning.

Great. Now I was going to have to spend the next few weeks convincing Sam that I hadn't been cruising malls or secretly logging on to the Internet to meet strange girls. He would never buy that a random girl just happened to want to talk to me for no apparent reason—even if she did announce to anyone within earshot that I didn't know her.

"Say no more. I'm out of here." Sam flashed me a thumbs-up and sauntered toward the other end of the lawn.

And then it was just us. The mystery girl and me. I crossed my arms in front of my chest and waited nervously for her to say something. I focused on her eyes, willing the butterflies that had for some reason formed in my stomach to go away.

"So . . . ," she said.

And with that one word I had the feeling that my life was about to change. I just didn't know what form that change would take. . . .

Seven

Nicole

"So . . ." I MANAGED to get out exactly one word before my mouth transformed itself into a giant cotton ball.

My hands were shaking, my palms were sweating, and my knees had become ill-formed lumps of jelly. *Get it together,* I ordered myself. *You're never going to convince him if he thinks you're a total psycho.*

But I couldn't help being overwhelmed with a kind of heady terror. This was the bravest (not to mention craziest) moment of my life. And Justin Banks was just so . . . cute. *Beyond cute,* I amended. He was even hotter than I remembered—which was saying a lot.

You're not asking Justin for a real date, I reminded myself. This would be a business/begging-for-mercy transaction only. Unless . . . well, unless he actually liked me.

"So . . ." Justin's voice interrupted my day-dream. "What do you want?"

I felt several pints of blood rushing to my face. I had to spit out my request *now.* If I didn't speak in the next second and a half, I knew I would simply turn and run.

"I want to take you to my prom tomorrow night," I blurted out. "The Union High senior prom."

He didn't even hesitate. Without taking one *moment* to consider my request, Justin started to shake his head. "Um . . . thanks. But no thanks."

My heart sank, and I felt like all of the air had left my lungs. That was it. A flat-out no. *This isn't happening,* I told myself. *You're so paranoid that you imagined his refusal before he even had a chance to properly respond.*

"Sorry," Justin added. And I knew that it *hadn't* been my imagination. He had turned me down outright.

"Oh. You have a girlfriend." That had to be the explanation, right? Otherwise he wouldn't have answered so quickly.

Besides, I was nuts to have thought for even a minute that a guy this gorgeous didn't have a girl-friend. Or two. Or three. He could probably date anyone he wanted to.

But again Justin shook his head. "Nope. No girlfriend."

No girlfriend? *What is up with this guy?* I wondered. In the next moment I realized the obvious truth. He hated me! Justin Banks had taken one look at my face and decided that I was the least prom-worthy girl on earth.

I wanted to turn around, sprint to the car, and peel out of the parking lot, never to be seen or heard from again. Justin Banks wasn't my dream guy—he was a jerk.

Then again, who could blame him for turning me down? He probably thought I was some insane stalker who had been secretly plotting to get him to take me to the prom for weeks. Of course, that description wasn't *entirely* inaccurate.

I couldn't walk away. Not with schoolwide humiliation staring me in the face on Monday morning. I opened my mouth and willed something brilliant, articulate, and witty to come out.

"Justin, you have to go to the prom with me," I exclaimed, sounding like an idiot. "I mean, you don't *have* to, obviously, but I really, really need you to be my date."

"Ah . . ." Justin's eyes were narrowed suspiciously, but he was listening. That was all that mattered.

"You see, there are these girls in my class who are really mean and nasty and stuck on themselves. And they came into the shop where I worked and started to make snide remarks about the fact that I didn't have a date for the prom. Of course, I *could* have a date, but, well, I'm picky." I took a deep breath. "But that's a whole other story."

"Uh-huh . . ." Justin was so beautiful—his picture in the yearbook definitely didn't do him justice.

You're babbling, I told myself. But I couldn't stop. Not now. "Anyway, you happened to be in the shop at the time, and I told them you were my prom date, and then you left, and I've been trying to find you ever since. Which wasn't easy . . ."

My mind seemed to separate from my body as I continued to tell Justin the story in one long, rambling run-on sentence. I could *see* myself standing there, talking like an idiot, but I was powerless to shut my mouth.

Finally Justin held up his hand, indicating that I should stop speaking. Abruptly I clamped my mouth shut. *Say yes,* I begged silently. *Please, say yes!*

"I hear what you're saying . . . but, uh, I don't know. . . ." He looked friendlier than he had a few minutes ago, but I could read on Justin's face that I hadn't won him over.

I glanced over at the parking lot, where Jane and Christy were hanging out next to the car. They nodded and smiled at me, sending silent messages of encouragement. I took a deep breath, preparing to take the final plunge.

"I'll give you fifty dollars to do me the favor of taking me to the prom," I announced. "And, of course, I'll pay for the entire evening."

Hey, what were a few more shifts at Claire's Boutique at this point? I was already going to have to work there until I was thirty to dig myself out of debt!

"I'll agree to take you to the prom," Justin said

after several *long* moments of utter silence. "But fifty dollars isn't what I want."

I raised an eyebrow, trying to keep focused on the matter at hand. But I was having a tough time thinking about anything besides how incredibly good Justin looked in the pair of worn khakis he was wearing. *Hello!*

"What *do* you want?" I asked. If he asked for a hundred, I was going to have to sell myself for medical experiments.

"I, uh, want to meet your friend." Justin's gaze traveled toward the parking lot, and he pointed at Christy.

So much for study dates, walking in the park, falling in love, and marital bliss. Only ten minutes into our relationship, Justin had already fallen for another girl. One of my best friends, to be exact. I willed away the sinking feeling in the pit of my stomach and forced myself to concentrate on the positive aspect of this conversation.

I'm going to get what I need, I thought. *That's all that matters.* Besides, I didn't even know this Justin Banks guy. Sure, he was gorgeous. But for all I knew, he had the personality of a Chia Pet. Anyway, the only reason I even wanted to go to the prom in the first place was to teach Rose, Madison, and the rest of their friends a lesson.

"No problem," I answered, managing to sound at least semicool and semicollected. "I'll get you a date with Christy."

Gulp. *Sorry, Christy,* I added silently. I wasn't in

the habit of promising virtual strangers that one of my friends would go on a date with them. But maybe I was doing Christy a favor. She'd said that her prom date, Jake, was the last guy she would want as a boyfriend. Why she was even going with Jake the Jerk (that was her name for him) was beyond Jane and me, but Christy wasn't forthcoming when we pressed her.

Anyway, what warm-blooded girl *wouldn't* want to go out with Justin?

I stuck out my hand. "So . . . it's a deal."

"Deal." Justin shook my hand, then looked into my eyes for slightly longer than was strictly necessary. "By the way—do you always use this kind of, uh, unorthodox method to get your dates?"

"It's not a real date," I reminded him. "And no, I don't."

Usually I don't use any methods at all, I added to myself. I literally couldn't remember the last time I had laid eyes on a guy I would want to walk in the moonlight with.

I pulled a small scrap of paper and a pen out of the back pocket of my blue jeans. "I'll pay—but you have to drive," I told Justin.

"Fair enough," he answered.

I wrote down my address on the slip of paper and placed it into Justin's outstretched hand. When my fingers brushed his skin, I felt an electric spark shoot all the way up my arm.

It's just nerves, I assured myself. *One little spark doesn't mean I'll be totally crushed if Justin and Christy fall in love and I have to spend the rest of my days watching them go gaga over each other the way Max and Jane do.* Right.

"Pick me up at seven o'clock," I added. "We're going to dinner at La Serenara before the dance."

Justin whistled. "La Serenara? That's the nicest restaurant in town."

Tell me something I don't know, I thought. "It's a long story," I pronounced. "And I doubt you want to hear me babble on about it for another fifteen minutes."

Justin laughed, and it was one of the most amazing sounds I had ever heard. Deep and rich and infectious. If only . . . well, if only.

I tore my gaze away from Justin's face, pivoted, and strode toward the parking lot. "See you tomorrow night!" I called over my shoulder.

"Wait!" Justin shouted. "I don't even know your name!"

I stopped in my tracks and turned around to look Justin in the eye. "Nicole Gilmore," I informed him.

Then I marched toward the car, resisting the urge to jump up and down or do a victory dance. *I did it!* Just now the enormity of my feat was sinking in. Mr. X was going to be my date to the Union High senior prom.

Even if Justin didn't like me, the prom was going to be a night I would never forget. And I was going to look absolutely fabulous in my strapless lavender gown—if I did say so myself!

Justin's Saturday To-Do List

A List of Annoying Tasks I Must Complete Before I Go to the Union High Senior Prom with a Virtual Stranger

1. Rent a tuxedo (otherwise known as a strait-jacket). Hope that I'm not stuck with something resembling a 1970s leisure suit.

2. Wash my car. The least I can do is shepherd this girl to her prom in a car that is not covered with dust and bird droppings.

3. Practice dance moves in the privacy of my own bedroom.

4. Shine my good shoes.

5. Shower. Use my superstrong deodorant soap to stave off any impending malodors.

6. Shave. Be particularly careful to avoid nicks and cuts since I don't want to go to the prom with bits of toilet paper stuck to my face (even if it's not a real date).

7. Contemplate splashing on a little aftershave. Reject the idea on the grounds that nobody but James Bond (007) can wear aftershave and not seem a bit cheesy.

8. Don tuxedo. Make sure that Star is on hand to help me with the bow tie and cummerbund.

9. Allow Star to take exactly one (1) picture of me in my tuxedo.

10. Pick up Nicole. Be sure to wipe my potentially sweaty palms on my pants leg before I go to her front door.

Eight

Justin

As I walked through the mall on Saturday morning, I was regretting the moment of weakness I had shown when I agreed to go to the prom with Nicole Gilmore. I didn't even know the girl. *Then again, who cares if I don't know her?* I thought. It's not like we were going on a real date. I was doing a favor for a stranger. Period.

"This is the place," Sam announced. "Joe's Tuxedos."

Sam, Star, and I stopped in front of the small shop. "With my luck all they'll have left is a powder blue tuxedo with a ruffle-front shirt," I commented.

"Well, *I* think you should rent a red cummerbund to go with your tux," Star informed me. "That'll make you totally stand out."

"I don't *want* to stand out," I retorted.

Bringing Star along on this little shopping excursion wouldn't have been my first choice. As soon as she had heard I was going to the Union High prom, my little sister had gone headfirst into hearts-and-flowers mode. She seemed to believe that going to a dance was up there with being crowned the king of England and winning the state lottery.

But I'd *had* to include Star in the outing. Dad worked every Saturday, and I had promised Star that I would take her to the mall to get a new pair of sneakers. Since I'd done so well in the patience department until she'd found her perfect dress and shoes and headband for her own dance, I was now her designated shopping partner. Besides, she had been so excited at the prospect of tagging along with Sam and me that I probably wouldn't have had the heart to say no even if I could have.

"Let's go behind door number one," Sam exclaimed. "If we don't get in there and get you a tux, you're going to have to go to the prom in jeans and a T-shirt."

"Fine with me," I muttered.

But I couldn't help feeling just a little excited as we walked into the shop. I hadn't been out of the house on a Saturday night in months. And there were only so many games of backgammon a guy could play with his dad before he went a little nuts.

"Welcome to Joe's Tuxedos," a small man with

wiry gray hair greeted us. "I'm Joe." He beamed at us and gave Star a wink. "How may I help you lovely people this afternoon?"

"I need a, uh, tux," I said. "I'm going to the prom tonight."

"Tonight!" Joe exclaimed. "Oh, my, we've got much work to do. Let's get started right away."

Star giggled as Joe took me by the arm and led me toward a small platform in front of a three-way mirror. I stood as still as a mannequin while Joe took my measurements.

"And who is the lucky girl?" Joe asked, tsking over the length of my arms.

"She's the most beautiful girl I've seen in ages," Sam informed him when I didn't say anything. "Aside from *my* girlfriend, of course."

"Do I get to meet her?" Star asked. "I really, really want to."

"No," I said firmly. The last thing I needed was to make this prom date into a family affair.

"I'll be right back," Joe said. "Don't go anywhere." He disappeared behind a red velvet curtain, still talking to himself.

"Your ugly brother got lucky with this one," Sam told Star. "For some crazy reason, she thinks he's hot stuff."

"Please, stop with the compliments." I stepped off the platform and paced nervously around the small shop. What if Joe didn't have a tux in my size? What would I do?

"I wonder who I'll go to *my* senior prom with,"

Star speculated. "Maybe Aaron Trent will take me. He's cute."

I rolled my eyes. "Easy there, little sister. You've got a few years before you've got to start shopping for a prom dress."

The velvet curtain opened with a flourish, and Joe emerged holding a perfectly pressed black tuxedo. "Ta da!" he exclaimed. "I have exactly what you need, young man."

"Phew." I had spent the last five minutes imagining myself driving from store to store, trying on ill-fitting tuxedos.

Joe placed the suit in my hands, then more or less shoved me into a tiny, brightly lit dressing room. I pulled off my clothes, praying that the pants of the tuxedo wouldn't come up to my knees.

"I'm so psyched you're going to the prom!" Star yelled from the other side of the door. "I'm sick of you skulking around the house every weekend!"

"Tell the whole world how you feel, Star," I called back. The girl certainly wasn't shy. I viewed the pants in the mirror. A perfect fit. *Joe will be proud,* I noted.

Still, it was great to see her so enthused. It was almost as if seeing me reenter the world at large was lifting a heavy burden from Star's shoulders. If I was getting on with my life, so could she.

Which is exactly why I'm not going to tell her the real reason I agreed to take Nicole to the prom, I thought, pulling on the trendy black tuxedo shirt. I didn't want to tell my sister about Christy, reminding her of the hospital and the waiting room and the doctors and the machines. She was too young to be dragged down with those kinds of images. I wanted her to forget them as quickly as possible.

I hadn't told Sam the real reason I was going to the Union High prom either. He had been a great friend—the best—throughout my mother's illness. But I didn't want to open up with him about all of this mushy stuff. It was too hard.

I just hope I can help Christy, I thought, buttoning the shirt. Or maybe . . . well, maybe I was hoping to help *myself.* As soon as I had seen Christy in Claire's Boutique, I had felt an urge to talk to her.

Speaking with someone who was going through what I had been through would allow me to let go of some of the pain, I theorized. It would be a catharsis. *And I have to let the pain go,* I realized. Wallowing in grief wasn't only harming me—it was probably hurting Dad and Star as well.

I finished buttoning the shirt, pulled on the jacket, and surveyed myself in the mirror. Wow. I looked halfway decent in this thing. I flashed a game-show-host grin in the mirror and did a miniature waltz around the dressing room. Not bad.

If I was totally honest with myself, I would have to admit that wanting to reach out to Christy wasn't the *only* reason I had acquiesced to Nicole's request. After all, I could have walked over to Nicole's car and introduced myself to Christy on the spot.

The truth was that I had admired how gutsy Ms. Nicole Gilmore had been. I could see how nervous she was when she walked up to me. Despite her casual bravado, her hands had been shaking, and she had seemed a little wobbly. But she had managed to walk up to a perfect stranger and ask him to the prom. And *then* she hadn't taken no for an answer. A person had to have confidence in the core of her being to pull off a move like that.

"Are you ever coming out of there?" Sam called. "If you stay in the dressing room much longer, Star is going to talk me into wearing a paisley bow tie with *my* tux at the Jefferson High prom next weekend."

I laughed. Somehow I didn't think Maya would appreciate that kind of apparel on Sam—even if she did love him for his quirky sense of humor. "I'm coming!"

I opened the door of the dressing room and stepped back into the shop. "Wow!" Star whispered. "You look like a movie star."

"Well, I don't know about that. . . ."

"She's right," Joe proclaimed. "I am a genius. I couldn't have done better with that tuxedo if I'd had a month to fit you."

"Thanks, Joe." I couldn't help grinning. *You'd think he was going to the prom,* I thought.

Sam got up from the small sofa he and Star had been lounging on while they waited for me to come out of the dressing room. He bowed deeply in front of Star and held out his hand.

"Madam, may I have this dance?" he asked, using a fake English accent.

Star giggled. "I would be delighted, kind sir," she responded, rising from the sofa.

Immediately Sam and Star began to do a variation of the fox-trot around the shop. "One, two, three, one, two, three," Sam chanted, spinning Star in small circles.

"Hey, you're not bad," I commented. *A lot better than I am,* I added to myself.

Sam grinned. "What I'm about to tell you can't go beyond these walls." He paused dramatically. "Maya has been making me take dance lessons."

I threw back my head, laughing. I couldn't remember the last time I had felt so free . . . so young. *It feels good,* I realized. I needed this.

I'm glad Nicole Gilmore appeared out of nowhere, I thought. A little dancing and some disgustingly sweet fruit punch were just what I needed. As long as I remembered to keep my hands off my gorgeous date.

I might be ready to go out and have a little fun. But nothing more. After tonight I would never see Nicole again.

Nicole's Preprom Checklist

Things I Must Accomplish before Justin Banks Arrives at My Door

1. Pluck eyebrows. (Note to self: Be sure to *carefully* follow plucking instructions from *Cosmo,* as I don't want to rip off half of my face in the process of trying to beautify my brows.)
2. Give myself a manicure and a pedicure. Be sure to allow ample drying time to avoid the kind of nail-polish fiasco that occurred when Jane, Christy, and I designated one Friday last winter as Home Spa Night.
3. Allot at least two hours for hair styling. Don't panic if the first three attempts at the upsweep fail. Practice makes perfect.
4. Allot one hour for makeup. Use Cindy Crawford's *Basic Face* to get that natural-but-beautiful look Cindy talked about on *Oprah.*
5. Have Mom help me steam press my perfect (and pricey) prom dress.
6. Assemble the whole package (dress, hair, and makeup). Add jewelry and Gwen's high heels.
7. Stare at myself in the mirror, searching for tiny flaws that will seem like major disfigurements.

8. Convince myself I look fine despite the major zit I can feel forming on my forehead. Who's going to let a minor skin irritation keep her from the prom?

9. Think of no less than three witty, cutting remarks to make to Rose and Madison, should the need arise.

10. When the doorbell rings, descend the stairs with the attitude and composure of the late Princess Diana.

Nine

Justin

WHY IS MY *heart beating so fast?* I asked myself as I stood outside the Gilmores' redbrick house. I was having a minor panic attack as I prepared to ring the doorbell.

Okay, so I was feeling a little nervous. But not because of *Nicole.* I just hadn't been on a date in a long time. Not since . . . well, not for a long time. I was out of practice. *How firmly do I shake her father's hand? Do I open her car door for her? Am I supposed to tell her she looks nice—even though this isn't a real date?*

I wasn't going to figure out the answers to these pressing questions by standing here. *Might as well go for it.* I pressed the bell, then took a step back from the door and waited.

A moment later the door opened. I found myself face-to-face with one of the tallest men I had ever seen. Just my luck. My first date in months, and her father was one of those totally intimidating types who liked to crush the fingers of his daughter's dates in his steel handshake.

"Uh, hi. I'm—I'm Justin Banks," I stammered.

Mr. Banks smiled, and all of my tension began to dissipate. His warm smile reminded me of a teddy bear's. "Great to meet you, Justin," he said, firmly shaking my hand. "Come on inside."

I walked into the house. "Hi, Justin," Mrs. Gilmore called, walking down the stairs. "Nicole will just be a minute."

"Nice to meet you, Mrs. Gilmore." I absorbed the motherly details of her presence, feeling instantly bathed in a warm glow.

We all stood there, looking at each other. Funny. Even though this wasn't a real date, I felt like a *real* guy, meeting a *real* girl's *real* parents. I sent a silent thanks to Joe for hooking me up with such a dignified-looking tuxedo. I would have been sweating like a pig if I'd had to stand here wearing some kind of magenta leisure suit. Instead I felt perfectly presentable.

"Nicole never told us how you two met," Mrs. Gilmore said in a soothing voice that reminded me of my own mom's. "Maybe you could fill us in while we wait for her."

"Oh. Um." What should I say? *Your daughter tracked me down in front of my high school* didn't seem appropriate. "It's really kind of a funny story—"

"Whoops. I guess we'll have to hear about it

later," Mr. Gilmore interrupted. "The girl of the hour is making her entrance."

I turned toward the staircase—and my breath caught in my throat. *Whoa!* Nicole looked . . . well, absolutely, in a word, *incredible.* She was wearing the same lavender dress she'd had on that day at the boutique. Only now she was wearing high heels and a sparkly necklace, and she had her hair piled atop her head in some kind of girl-hairdo thing, complete with pink roses. And how was it possible that I hadn't noticed those perfect cheekbones the first time I had laid eyes on her?

"Hey, Justin," Nicole greeted me as she glided down the stairs as if she were walking on air rather than four-inch heels.

"Uh, hi." I blanked. *Name. Name. Name.* "Nicole!" I blurted out finally. Phew. Forgetting their daughter's name wasn't the impression I wanted to make with the Gilmores. *Not that it matters,* I amended.

"You look great," I told Nicole as she reached the bottom of the stairs. Hey, it would have been rude just to stand there mute.

"Honey, you're absolutely gorgeous," Mrs. Gilmore gushed. "Dad and I want to get a picture of you and Justin before you go off and have a great time."

"Mom, no pictures!" Nicole responded. She raised her eyebrows in my direction and flashed me an apologetic smile.

Mrs. Gilmore frowned. "But we need a photograph!"

"Of course we do," I added, stepping forward. "I mean, it's not a prom without a picture, right?"

Could I have sounded any stupider? This was exactly the kind of awkward moment that made guys' palms sweat. And it was about to get worse—because it was almost time for the Pinning of the Corsage.

I held out the small box that contained the single white rose that Star had convinced me to buy for Nicole this afternoon. My sister had simply refused to leave the mall until I had purchased a corsage for my prom date.

Nicole took the rose out of the box, then handed it to me. "Do you, uh, want to put it on for me?" she asked.

I nodded, and my palms started to sweat, right on cue. The corsage felt tiny in my big hands, and I was half afraid that I was going to gouge Nicole with the pins the florist had given me.

"Got it," I announced finally, breathing a sigh of relief.

"Good job," Nicole complimented me. She touched the flower lightly, her fingers moving like a butterfly's wings.

"Thanks." I brushed my palms against the legs of my pants and followed Nicole and her parents into their spacious living room. Mrs. Gilmore herded Nicole and me toward the fireplace.

Mrs. Gilmore put a small, automatic camera up to her eye. "Stand a little closer together," she instructed, peering through the lens.

I inched closer to Nicole and placed my arm around her slender waist. The fabric of her dress was cool against my hand, but I couldn't help notice the slight tingle that traveled up my arm. *It's been a long time since I touched a girl,* I realized.

"Smile!" Mr. Gilmore ordered.

Dutifully Nicole and I grinned for the camera. A moment later the flash went off.

"Perfect!" Mrs. Gilmore exclaimed. "Now we just need one more—for Justin's family."

Nicole and I smiled again, and Mrs. Gilmore took the photograph. "Let's get out of here," Nicole whispered. Parent time was now over, and the night was officially about to begin.

"I'm ready when you are," I answered. I followed Nicole out of the living room toward the front door.

"Bye, Mom. Bye, Dad." She kissed each of her parents on the cheek.

"It was nice to meet you," I told Mr. and Mrs. Gilmore, reaching out to shake Nicole's dad's hand again.

"Have fun, kids," Mrs. Gilmore called.

"Don't stay out too late," Mr. Gilmore added. "And no drinking and driving. Period."

"We *know,* Dad." Nicole rolled her eyes at me as I pulled open the front door.

Seconds later we were outside, surrounded by the warm spring air. I inhaled deeply, appreciating the scent of the honeysuckle bushes that lined one side of the Gilmores' yard. I had a good feeling about tonight. It was going to be fun.

"Hey, thanks for the corsage," Nicole said as soon as the door shut behind us. "Even though this isn't a real date, I appreciate the niceties."

"Oh . . . right, no problem." Oops. For a moment I had almost forgotten that this *wasn't* a real date.

The dress, the flowers, the picture, the parents—the evening had all of the ingredients of an actual, real-life date. *But I'm glad it's not,* I reminded myself. *I never would have agreed to a real date.*

But Nicole was a beautiful, intelligent girl. I was going to have to be careful tonight . . . very, very careful.

Ten

Nicole

BY THE TIME Justin and I strolled into La Serenara for our dinner reservation, I felt at least halfway confident about walking in the super-high heels I had borrowed from Gwen. With any luck, I wouldn't trip on the way to our table.

"It smells awesome in here," Justin commented, inhaling deeply. "I feel like a young millionaire, out on the town."

"I know what you mean," I answered, clutching his arm for support as I walked up the small set of steps that led to the main dining room.

Sure, after tonight I would be a pauper, toiling for weeks on end to dig myself out of debt. But for this one night I felt like a princess. I had it all—the gown, the guy, the corsage. This might be a grand illusion, but it *felt* real.

"Two for dinner," I said to the maitre d'. "The name is Gilmore."

He scanned the list of names in front of him, then gave us a warm smile. "Ah, yes. Prom night, yes?"

"Actually, we're going to a monster-truck rally," I joked, squeezing Justin's arm.

The maitre d' fluttered his eyelashes. "Young love," he said with a sigh. "So tender, so sweet, so light at heart."

"And so hungry," Justin added.

"But of course." The man pivoted toward the main dining room. "Follow me."

As we wended our way through the elegant, dimly lit restaurant, I scanned the tables for Madison and Rose. Of course, if they were there, I probably wouldn't have had to *look* for them—I would have heard the girls' grating, shrill giggles from halfway down the block.

There was no sign of Rose and Madison or their dates. But I had no doubt that they would turn up eventually. I would simply bide my time until it was time to show off the fact that I had the hottest date around.

We stopped in front of a small table next to a huge window, and Justin pulled out my chair. "Thank you," I said, wishing more than ever that the class jerks were there to see Nicole Gilmore being treated like a prom queen.

"My pleasure, Nicole." His deep, slightly husky voice sent a small, almost imperceptible shiver up my spine.

Justin slid into his seat and immediately picked up the pale blue linen napkin that was resting on top of the table. He put the napkin in his lap, then straightened the array of silverware placed in front of him. Wow. The guy was gorgeous *and* well mannered. A rare combination in any high-school boy.

Thank goodness Justin's not some total louse, I thought. *I really lucked out.* The truth was that I had picked Justin Banks as a prom date completely at random. I had been in the throes of desperation, and he had been the cutest guy in a three-shop radius. But I had had zero knowledge that he wasn't a complete jerk. *Phew!* A date who was a complete embarrassment was worse than no date at all. Any girl with a modicum of self-respect knew that much.

"Have you ever been here before?" Justin asked, opening his menu.

I shook my head. "Nope. But I've heard the food is amazing."

I stared at the menu, but I wasn't reading any of the words. Instead I was racking my brain for something else to say. *Nice weather we're having* was one totally dull option. Or I could go the twenty-questions route. *What's your favorite color? Do you have a middle name? Have you figured out what you're going to major in at college?*

But I didn't want to bore Justin to sleep with typical first-date conversation (not that I'd had many first dates). I wanted to be charming and witty and intelligent. Basically I wanted to prove to the guy that I wasn't a complete psycho who could only get a date by hunting someone down through their yearbook photo—even if that was sort of the truth.

"Have you decided what to order?" Justin asked, breaking the silence.

"Not yet." *Actually, I haven't even read the first item on the menu,* I added silently. "Everything looks so good, I don't know what I want."

Justin coughed. "Um . . . yeah. The entrées sound . . . interesting."

I forced myself to focus on the menu, quickly reading the description of each dish. My eyebrows shot up as I absorbed the contents of various entrées. These weren't just fancy pasta dishes or T-bone steaks.

"The goat brain looks especially tasty," I commented dryly.

Justin nodded solemnly. "Yes, I'm always tempted to order brains. But tonight I may be adventurous and go for the tongue."

"Are you sure?" I asked, struggling not to laugh. "Because I've always found that the walnut glaze the tongue is served with can be a bit heavy—not conducive to dancing."

"You've got a good point, Nic," Justin responded with a grin. "On second thought, I think I'll order the chicken."

Nic. He called me Nic. "What an amazing coincidence!" I exclaimed. "I've been craving chicken all day."

Justin closed his menu. "I guess we're not cut out for haute cuisine."

"I beg to differ," I countered. "After all, we're going to get the escargot for an appetizer."

"We are?" Justin asked, his face a study in snail phobia.

"Did I say 'escargot'?" I asked, wide-eyed. "I *meant* to say 'fried zucchini sticks.'"

Justin laughed, and I couldn't help but notice that his smile was one of the warmest I had ever seen. And his eyes were like laser beams as he gazed at me from the other side of the tiny table.

"If you're with me . . . I've got a radical idea," Justin announced. "But feel free to wimp out if you're not up for the challenge."

"I'm *always* up for a challenge," I assured him. "What is it?"

"Let's order the escargot. I'll eat snail meat if you will."

"I'm with you," I responded. "After all, we don't want to disappoint our waiter."

As if on cue, a waiter wearing a white tuxedo appeared beside our table. "Have mademoiselle and monsieur decided?" he asked with a French accent.

Justin started to give the waiter our order, and I found myself on the verge of a hysterical giggling fit. I picked up my napkin from my lap and held it over my mouth, feeling like a seven-year-old trying not to laugh during a church service.

When the waiter finally walked away, Justin gave me a mock glare. "You were *no* help," he accused me. "I can't take you anywhere."

83

I couldn't help myself. I started to giggle. Within seconds Justin was laughing even louder than I was.

"We have to be *serious*," I proclaimed. "This is a *serious* establishment." But just looking across the table at Justin was making me giggle.

"You're right," Justin answered. "This is no time for joking around. We're surrounded by so-phisticated people eating sophisticated meals . . . consisting of cow intestines."

As I grinned at Justin, I caught sight of a flash of pale pink taffeta in my peripheral vision. I blinked, then turned my head. Madison and Rose were cruising through La Serenara in their pairs of five-inch heels as if they walked the runways in Milan every day.

Whoa. *I forgot they were coming,* I realized. During the last twenty minutes it hadn't occurred to me even once to check the door for the Witch Brigade's grand entrance. I had been having such a good time that I had lost sight of the evening's true mission—to prove to those snobs that I could get the best-looking date ever.

I reached across the table and tapped Justin's forearm. "There are the girls I was telling you about," I whispered. "The ones who inspired me to track you down and beg you to be here tonight."

Justin twisted around in his chair. "Where?"

"Don't look!" I hissed. "Just act like you're in love with me." I paused, realizing that more or less barking at a guy in order to get him to cozy up wasn't the best idea in the world. "Please."

"Gotcha." Justin scooted his chair around the table so that it was next to mine.

The next thing I knew, he had slipped his arm around my shoulders, and he was holding me close. He tilted his head so that his lips were just millimeters from my ear.

"How's this?" he whispered. "Should I actually pull you into my lap—or do you think they're getting the picture?"

Justin's words washed over me like liquid fire. I felt blood rushing to my face at a rate of approximately ten liters per second, and I felt like I wasn't going to be able to breathe for the rest of the night. *It's just nerves,* I assured myself. *You're feeling hypersensitive because this is your big moment with Rose and Madison.*

"This is perfect," I whispered back. "Keep it up."

I shifted my body so that I was resting against Justin's torso, virtually nestled in his arms. Then I gazed across the room until Rose and Madison caught my glance. *Eat your hearts out,* I told them silently, hoping the mental telepathy found its way into their heads.

I watched as each girl studied Justin. *That's right—he's gorgeous.* After several long seconds the girls nudged each other. Madison raised her eyebrows and mimed that she was tipping her hat to me. Rose flashed a discreet thumbs-up sign.

I wanted to glare at the horrible twosome. But I couldn't control the grin that was spreading across my face. I had accomplished my goal. Rose and Madison were admitting defeat, and I had come out on top.

"So, what's the verdict?" Justin asked quietly. "Am I up to par?"

I shifted in my seat again so that I could look him in his eyes. "You're *more* than acceptable," I assured him. "With your help I have successfully avoided having prom night be the worst night of my life."

I wished I had the words to express what that meant to me. For all of high school I had resisted the urge to do whatever stupid things were necessary to "fit in" with the right crowd. I had turned down dates offered by mindless jocks, refused to be drawn into debates about Nike versus Reebok sneakers, and hadn't even been tempted to try out for the cheerleading squad.

But tonight I had shown, in some small way, that I *could* have done any of those things. I had maintained my integrity for four years, and though it was dumb of me to care, now girls like Rose and Madison were forced to realize that I wasn't a loser. I was just . . . me. Well, I was me *plus* one great date.

"Thank you," I told Justin. "This night means a lot to me—for a lot of different reasons that I won't bore you with."

"You're welcome," he answered. "For a lot of different reasons that I won't bore *you* with."

Huh. *Interesting response,* I noted. I was dying to

ask Justin to expand on his cryptic statement, but I sensed that he didn't want me to pry. And then it came to me. *Duh.* He was referring to Christy.

He's psyched that I'm going to give him an introduction to her—and he probably knows that it won't hurt her opinion of him that he's dressed to the nth degree in that tuxedo.

"Do you want me to go back to my side of the table now?" Justin asked, breaking into my thoughts. "Or should we continue the show for a few more minutes?"

"Um . . . let's let them observe our state of romantic bliss for a little while longer," I suggested. "You know, to make sure they get the point."

"No problem." Justin adjusted his position so that one hand rested on my waist while the other rested lightly against mine on top of the table.

There was simply no getting around it. Every time Justin's skin came into contact with mine, I felt a tingle travel the length of my entire body. This wasn't a case of nerves—it was pure, animal attraction.

Suddenly I didn't care about Madison or Rose or any of their friends. They had stopped being an issue. Now I had a bigger problem than the (now defunct) possibility of being humiliated at the senior prom. A much bigger problem.

I'm falling for Justin, I admitted to myself. And there was zero chance that he would ever return my feelings. The only reason Justin had agreed to go on this nondate was that he wanted the opportunity to meet Christy. He had made it perfectly clear that he never would have been my date just because he *wanted* to be.

The waiter appeared with our escargot, and Justin moved back to his side of the table. My waist and hand felt bare now that his fingers were no longer brushing against my skin.

"It's our moment of truth," Justin commented. "To snail or not to snail, that is the question."

I stifled a huge, dramatic sigh. After years of avoiding dates with total jerks, I had stumbled on a diamond in the proverbial rough. And I couldn't have him.

I glanced at the gray lumps sitting on the tiny plate in front of me. *I know how you guys feel,* I thought. Unwanted, icky, slimy . . . the list went on.

Yes, I had completed the mission I had set for myself. But it wasn't enough anymore. It wasn't *nearly* enough.

Eleven

Nicole

THE PARKING LOT at Union High was almost full by the time Justin and I arrived for the prom. Clearly the entire senior class had decided to show up for this age-old rite of passage.

"I should warn you right now that I'm not the greatest dancer," Justin said as we walked across the parking lot toward the gym. "In fact, my little sister spent half the afternoon trying to give me a crash course."

"That's too bad," I joked. "I'm the Union High lambada champion."

At the door of the gymnasium I handed our prom tickets to Mrs. Learner, the home-economics teacher. "Have a wonderful time," she sang out. "It's a magical night."

I rolled my eyes at her cheesy enthusiasm, but as

we walked into the prom, I had to admit to myself that there *was* something magical about the transformation that the prom committee had executed in the high-school gym.

We were staring at a winter wonderland in the middle of May, complete with twinkling lights, fake snow, and dozens and dozens of red poinsettia plants. The bleachers were gone. In their place were tiny wrought-iron tables with matching chairs. A disco ball hanging from the ceiling bathed the huge room in otherworldly light.

"Nice!" Justin exclaimed. "You guys really know how to throw a party."

"Yeah . . . I guess we do." Not that I could take any of the credit. I would have laughed in the face of anyone who had tried to convince me to help with the prom decorations. But the joke would have been on me. Because this place was amazing.

I led Justin into the crowd, still not quite able to absorb that I was actually here. *I can't believe I almost missed this,* I thought. Now that I could hear the music and the laughter and see the hundreds of beautiful dresses and elegant tuxedos, I realized that the prom really *was* an essential part of the high-school experience. It was sort of a symbol of our impending transition from teenagedom to adulthood.

In a weird way Rose and Madison had done me a huge favor when they had shoved their snobby attitude at me. If those girls hadn't given me the challenge of a lifetime, I never would have taken it upon myself to find a date to the dance. I would have scorned the whole event, then made snide comments when Christy and Jane filled me in on the details on Monday.

But this night beat baby-sitting the Fiedler twins by a mile. True, my feet were already starting to ache, and I was fairly sure that mascara was covering at least half of my face. But it was better than burning my finger on the Fiedlers' toaster oven in a misguided attempt to make the twins s'mores. In fact, it was pretty amazing.

"It feels good to be out!" Justin shouted over the music. "Thank you!"

It feels good to be out? What did that mean, exactly? A guy like Justin was probably out every Friday and Saturday night. I wouldn't have been surprised to learn that ten different girls from ten different schools had asked him to the prom. He was, after all, the African American version of Cinderella's Prince Charming.

But every girl couldn't provide what I could. Justin wanted to meet Christy, and that was why he was here. It was a fact that I was going to have to repeat to myself over and over again for the rest of the night.

And I had every intention of keeping my end of the bargain. Justin had shown up, and he had more than fulfilled his end of our deal. It wasn't as if a corsage and a cuddling session at the restaurant had been part of our contract.

Now it's my job to introduce him to Christy, I realized.

After that, Justin and I would be even. We could go our separate ways, not owing each other a thing. The thought filled me with sadness, but I shoved aside the wistful longing that was washing over me.

I was going to enjoy my evening—even if it wasn't going to end with the hearts and music (and good-night kiss) that would have completed a perfect picture. Being at the prom with Mr. Gorgeous was what I had wanted. And that's what I had gotten. To have expected more would be . . . greedy.

"Nicole!" I heard Jane call my name before I actually caught sight of her. But as she emerged from the crowd, I whistled.

In a sleeveless pale blue silk dress, Jane looked absolutely beautiful. Her blond hair was swept into a French twist, and she wore a choker made of crystals around her long, slender neck.

"You look like a supermodel." I gave her a big hug and grinned at Max, who was standing a few feet away in a black tuxedo.

I still hadn't spotted Christy and her date, Jake, but I had no doubt that they were around here somewhere. And Jane was the ideal source for that particular bit of information.

"So do you," Jane assured me. "And your date ain't half bad either," she added, lowering her voice.

I felt a pang. If only Justin were a real date. Then I would be as radiant as Jane was. Instead I felt like something of a fraud. I was parading Justin around as if he were the love of my life when he was really nothing more than a hired helper.

Behind Jane's shoulder I saw that Justin and Max were introducing themselves to each other. They looked like they were getting along, but I didn't know how much longer Justin would be willing to wait before he expected the big introduction.

"Nicole, how come you never told anyone you had a boyfriend?" Max asked. "Jane and I could have been going on double dates with you guys if you hadn't kept Justin a secret."

"Uh . . . l-long story," I stammered.

"Why don't we go get the prom queens some sickeningly sweet punch?" Justin suggested to Max. "I still have the taste of snail in my mouth."

"Good idea!" Jane piped up. "Nic and I need to talk. I mean, we need to freshen up our makeup."

"Don't spend all night in the girls' room," Max said, pulling Jane close. "I want to get out on the dance floor and hold you in my arms."

I was practically drooling as I watched Max and Jane exchange a long kiss. *You'd think they were saying good-bye for a month—not ten minutes,* I thought, hating the fact that I was feeling the tiniest bit jealous of their fairy-tale romance.

"I'll, um, see you in a few," Justin said in a way that let me know he was feeling as awkward as I was about viewing this oh-so-public display of affection.

After what seemed like an hour, Jane and Max finally broke apart from each other. Max gave Jane one last, yearning glance, then disappeared into a throng of prom goers with Justin following close behind.

Jane grabbed my arm and pulled me in the direction of the bathroom. "I want to hear everything," she informed me. "And don't leave out one single second of the action."

I sighed. Unfortunately, there wasn't "everything" to tell. In reality, there wasn't *anything* to tell. On the outside, my night was a total triumph. But inside, I was feeling turmoil.

And if I knew Jane as well as I thought I did, then there was almost no doubt that by the end of our imminent girl-to-girl rap session, my emotions were going to be laid out on the bathroom floor in a big, messy heap of confusion. I could hardly wait.

"Max has kissed me so many times tonight that I've already redone my lipstick three times," Jane said giddily as we walked into the packed women's locker room at the far end of the gymnasium. "Uh-oh," she added, turning to me. "I'm being totally sickening again, aren't I?"

I laughed and nodded. "You two are a great couple," I told her. "It's like you were made for each other."

For a brief moment I fantasized that it was Jane who was telling *me* that Justin and I were made for each other. I imagined my coy smile and fluttering eyelashes as I shyly agreed with her assessment. *It must be amazing to find a person who can make you feel like that,* I thought wistfully.

"Tell me all about dinner," Jane ordered, pulling a lipstick out of the tiny pale blue handbag she had bought to go with her dress. "How are things going with you and Mr. Wonderful?"

I uncapped a tube of mascara and leaned close to the mirror. There were globs of black gunk all over my lashes. Whoops. Apparently my makeup job had been far from expert.

"Nicole, I'm dying for details!" Jane insisted. "Tell me about La Serenara—and Justin."

I shrugged, staring at myself in the mirror. "There's nothing to tell. He's a guy, he showed up, Rose and Madison saw us. Mission accomplished."

Jane caught my gaze in the mirror. "That's *it*? Mission accomplished?"

"Yeah. I mean, I guess Justin is nice enough, but he's really not my type." I concentrated on applying a new coat of mascara in order to keep a telltale quiver out of my voice. "To tell you the truth, he's sort of a bore."

Jane finished her fresh lipstick job and stepped away from the mirror. "He's *boring*?" she asked, sounding suspicious. "Justin seems like a lot of things—gorgeous, sweet, funny, charming. But I wouldn't put 'boring' on the list."

"I just spent two hours with the guy, Jane," I replied huffily. "If I say he's boring, he's boring."

"Then how come I could see your toothpaste smile from all the way across the dance floor the second you walked into the prom?" she asked.

I shrugged again. "I don't know. . . . Maybe I was thinking about something funny I saw on TV last night."

My excuses sounded lame even to me. But as soon as I admitted out loud just how much I really did like Justin, my feelings would become real. And that was the last thing I wanted.

Jane gave me one of those looks that said I-don't-believe-a-word-you're-saying-so-don't-even-try-to-lie-to-me. "Well, according to my extrasensory perception, you *do* like Justin," she informed me. "And judging from the way he was looking at you, I think he likes you too. A lot."

I slipped the mascara back into my purse, giving up the idea of achieving the perfect cover-girl lashes. "Can we drop this?" I pleaded. "Justin and I are at the prom together. That's it—end of story."

Jane shook her head. "I don't get it, Nic. You should be totally psyched . . . but you seem upset." She paused. "You're not telling me something—what is it?"

I bit my lip. I wasn't proud of the fact that I had used the promise of meeting Christy to entice Justin to go to the prom with me. So far, I had kept the deal a secret. But it was going to come out eventually. And now seemed like as good a time as any to reveal the bargain I had made with Justin. Besides, telling Jane the truth would definitely put an end to her inquisition.

"Justin didn't agree to go to the prom with me because he actually wanted to be my date," I admitted. "The first time I asked him, he told me no, flat out."

"So?" Jane asked. "That doesn't mean he didn't

change his mind. I mean, he's here, isn't he?"

"He's only here because I promised him something in return for the favor of helping me avert total social ruin."

Jane looked concerned. "What did you promise?"

"I promised that I would introduce him to Christy," I informed her. "Because that's what he wanted. We were standing in front of his high school, and Justin said he would accompany me to the dance on only one condition—that I introduce him to my friend. Then he pointed to Christy."

"Huh." Jane was quiet for a few moments, contemplating this new piece of information. "Well . . . maybe there's an explanation. You could have misinterpreted what Justin meant by that."

I shook my head. "I know what I heard, Jane. He likes Christy—not me."

I tried to ignore the way my guts were twisting into a big, tight knot. This wasn't the time to fall apart because some guy I barely knew didn't think I was the girl of his dreams. I was determined to have a good time tonight—no matter what the circumstances.

"Where is Christy anyway?" I asked Jane, hoping my tone sounded as upbeat as I wanted it to. "I haven't seen her since we got here."

"I don't know," Jane responded. "I haven't seen her since we first arrived."

"Weird. I thought she'd spend all of prom in the bathroom, avoiding Jake. I know she was dreading having to spend the whole evening with the guy."

Christy had made it clear that Jake wasn't boyfriend material. She found him rude, obnoxious, and self-centered. But for some reason that Jane and I hadn't totally figured out, our friend had agreed to go to the prom with the guy anyway.

Jane snapped her fingers. "Hey, I just had a brilliant idea."

"What?" I asked. Maybe she had some new insight into the dubious art of mascara application.

"Why don't you avoid introducing Justin to Christy for as long as possible?" she suggested. "Maybe Justin will fall for you in the meantime."

It was a tempting notion. After all, it wasn't as if Justin and I weren't getting along. He had seemed to enjoy our dinner . . . and he *had* said I looked pretty in my dress.

But no. It wouldn't be right to try to manipulate Justin like that. He had held up his end of the bargain, and it wasn't fair for me to renege on *my* promise. Besides, if Justin had decided he liked me, he could have told me to forget about the introduction to Christy. And he had said no such thing.

Finally I shook my head. "Nope. A deal is a deal."

Jane sighed. "I'm really sorry, Nic. I wish tonight had turned out differently for you."

I smiled. "Hey, it's no big deal," I lied. "Let's get back out there—you've got an appointment to slow dance with your adorable boyfriend."

I followed Jane out of the bathroom, willing myself back into the great mood I had been in at La

Serenara. The last thing I wanted was for Justin to sense that his desire to go out with one of my best friends was bringing me down. The whole point of tonight had been to *avoid* embarrassment—not to invite it.

As soon as were outside the locker room, Jane made a beeline for Max. I didn't blame her. This was probably the most romantic night of her life. I, on the other hand, had work to do.

I stood on my tiptoes and scanned the dance floor. After several seconds I finally spotted Christy. She was in the middle of the crowd, dancing with Jake. *Good, I can get this stupid introduction out of the way . . . and at least try to enjoy the rest of the night.*

Luckily at the exact moment that I saw Jake and Christy, I noticed that Justin was heading in my direction.

"There you are!" Justin exclaimed, handing me a cup of now lukewarm punch. "I thought you'd decided to ditch me by climbing out of the bathroom window."

I set the punch down on a nearby table and grabbed Justin's hand. "Actually, I've been hard at work," I told him.

He raised his eyebrows. "I don't get it."

"Let's go," I said, pulling Justin toward the dance floor. "I'm about to hold up my end of this bargain." *And it's going to break my heart . . .*

Twelve

Justin

I'M GOING TO hold up my end of this bargain. Nicole's
words echoed through my brain as she pulled me
toward the dance floor. I knew what she was planning to do. Nicole was going to introduce me to
Christy, just as I had asked her to do.

But now wasn't the right time. I had noticed
Christy dancing with her date as I had been wan-
dering around the prom with Nicole's glass of
punch. As soon as I had seen her, I had stood at the
edge of the crowd and watched Christy.

She had looked happy and carefree, her hair
flying around her head as she danced to a retro
seventies tune. And as I found her again with my
gaze, I saw that she still looked like she was having a great time. The haunted look in her eyes
that I had recognized that day in front of Jefferson

101

High was gone, and she was laughing.

My whole plan has been sort of off, I realized, watching Christy's date dip her almost to the floor. She obviously hadn't recognized me from the hospital. She hadn't even blinked the last two times I had seen her.

And the night of the girl's senior prom wasn't exactly the best time to walk up to her and say, "Hey, I recognize you from the cancer ward. Want to get together and form a support group?"

Nope. Now was not the appropriate time to make Christy's acquaintance. She seemed happy, and I didn't want to remind her of the illness that was undoubtedly the most painful thing in her life. Not now.

I pulled Nicole to a stop, trying not to notice how great her soft hand felt inside mine. *Putting off the introduction to Christy isn't entirely for Christy's sake,* I realized.

"Where are we going?" Nicole asked as I led her back to the edge of the crowd. "Christy is *that* way," she added, pointing toward her friend.

"I just want to talk to you for a second," I explained. "Hold up."

For the first time in a long time I felt like a regular guy. The kind who laughed and danced and gave my date little paper cups filled with nasty fruit punch. It was a foreign sensation. But . . . well, it was *fun.* And I didn't want it to end. Not yet.

"What's wrong?" Nicole asked. "This is your big moment."

"I, uh . . ." What was I going to say, exactly? It wasn't as if I had filled Nicole in on *why* I wanted to meet her friend. She was completely in the dark.

"You, uh, *what?*" she asked, sounding more than a little annoyed.

"I noticed that Christy looks pretty involved in what she's doing," I said, gesturing toward the middle of the dance floor, where Christy's date was twirling her around in some kind of swing move. "Maybe now isn't the best time to interrupt her."

Nicole dropped my hand. "Whatever you say, Justin. It's your call."

Why did she sound mad? It was almost as if Nicole couldn't *wait* to get rid of me. *She wants to dump me off on her friend now that I've done my duty,* I thought, feeling strangely let down.

But I wasn't ready to let Nicole off the hook. She had asked me to be her date to the prom, and that's exactly what I was being. Even if the so-called date was more than a little unconventional. I wasn't going to be gotten rid of—not yet anyway.

"Why don't we get out on the dance floor ourselves?" I suggested. "Those girls you were trying to impress would probably think it was pretty weird if you didn't even dance with your date."

Nicole's eyes lit up. "Good point," she proclaimed. "Besides, there's no reason we can't have some fun together. 'No dancing' wasn't written into the bylaws of our agreement."

"So what's it going to be?" I asked. "The foxtrot or the cha-cha-cha?"

Nicole grinned. "I don't think either of those dances is quite right for this tune. Why don't we get out there and let our spirits move us?" she suggested. "But no *Saturday Night Fever* moves. We've got a reputation as the coolest couple at the prom to uphold."

I clasped Nicole's hand in mine again, surprised at how easy it was to talk to her. A lot of girls needed to hear a constant stream of compliments in order to have a good time, but Nicole was all about witty banter and intelligent conversation. It was a nice change from . . . what I had been used to in the past.

We stopped in the middle of the dance floor, directly under the disco ball. "Do you think we're front and center enough?" I asked, semishouting over the band's rendition of "Brick House." "We wouldn't want your 'friends' to miss the show."

"This is a great spot," Nicole assured me. "As long as I don't fall on my butt in front of the entire senior class."

"If either of us hits the floor, we'll make it look like a never-before-seen dance move," I told her.

Just as Nicole and I started to dance, "Brick House" came to an abrupt stop. A moment later the band launched into a version of some slow song that I had heard on the radio but never bothered to pay attention to. *Uh-oh, it looks like we're in for a full-contact dance number,* I thought. Was I ready for this?

Nicole seemed to sense my hesitancy. "Why don't we sit this one out?" she suggested. "This is a song for people on *real* dates."

I was torn between wanting nothing more than to slide my hands around Nicole's waist and feeling terrified of what dancing with her *that* way might do to me. But in the next second the decision was made for me. I saw one of the girls from the restaurant staring at us from several yards away.

I didn't even bother to respond to what Nicole had said. I simply stepped forward and took her in my arms. For a split second Nicole looked confused. Then she melted into my embrace, and we began to sway to the soft, sultry music.

"This is nice," Nicole murmured quietly. "I feel like this is the kind of moment the prom was invented for." She paused. "I mean, you know, if I were into that kind of thing."

I nodded, too distracted by the softness of Nicole's skin to reply. I inhaled deeply, absorbing the scent of her perfume, the silky texture of her hair, the delicate fabric of her long, sexy dress. All of my senses had shifted into high gear as I became more and more tantalized by the essence of the girl I held in my arms.

Gently I pulled Nicole even closer, and she rested her head against the lapel of my tuxedo jacket. When was the last time I had felt like this? It had been so long that it was difficult to remember that I had ever been the kind of guy who delighted in the soft touch of a beautiful girl.

The homecoming dance sophomore year with Laurie, I remembered. That was the last time I had allowed myself to be swept away by the presence of another human being. Suddenly images of Laurie washed through my consciousness. I saw her at the school fair, eating cotton candy. And sitting beside me in the car, singing along to the radio.

And then I saw her face—cold, distant, unknowable. In an instant I felt gripped in a familiar sense of pain and longing. *No!* I shouted to myself. *No!*

I took ahold of Nicole's arms and pushed her away. I had to get out of here. I didn't want to be surrounded by smiling faces and shrill laughter. I needed to be alone, away from Nicole.

"I, uh, need to get some air," I told her, already several feet away from her still outstretched arms. "I'll catch up with you later."

I ignored the hurt look on her face and turned away. I pushed my way through the dancing couples, desperate to find that huge steel door that led to freedom—and peace. Striding through the made-over gymnasium, I kept my gaze fixed on the far side of the door. It was imperative that I *not* catch sight of Nicole again.

After what felt like forever but was probably less than forty-five seconds, I found myself in front of the entrance to the prom. I walked straight past the grinning face of the dance chaperon and pushed on the door.

A moment later I was bathed in fresh spring air. The prom seemed a million miles away as I jogged across the parking lot, searching for a quiet place where I could be alone.

I can't believe I did that, I thought, chastising my

weakness. For a few minutes—maybe even for a few hours—I had forgotten my promise to myself. I had allowed Nicole to get under my skin, into my brain.

I let myself start to fall for her, I realized, mentally cursing the fact that I had ever agreed to this non-date to the prom. I should have realized the moment I saw Nicole that it would be next to impossible to maintain the cordial-yet-distant air of friendly acquaintances.

I should have recognized the temptation that Nicole Gilmore represented and stayed as far away from her as humanly possible. *But it's not too late to save myself.* I would forget the smell of her hair, the feel of her skin, the bright light of her smile. I would shut those qualities out of my mind, where they would stay buried forever.

I simply couldn't afford to let myself fall for another girl. No matter how much I wanted to.

Thirteen

Nicole

I STOOD IN the middle of the dance floor, staring at the space that Justin had filled just moments ago. What had happened? I felt like I had entered some episode of *The Twilight Zone*. One second I had been slow dancing with my date, then the next second he had vanished into thin air.

He hates me, I thought. *I repulse him*. I blinked back tears as I pushed my way through the crowded dance floor. This was the worst. Tonight had been a roller coaster—up and down, up and down, up and down. But I felt like the ride had come to a screeching halt, and my heart had been left on one of the loopity loops.

I had been upset earlier, after I realized that Justin was a great guy who was interested in my friend rather than me. But I had been handling that emotion with a certain amount of dignity. I had told myself that the end of my senior year was a lousy time to fall in love anyway. I had five exams to study for, two papers to write, graduation to prepare for. Who had time for dates?

Had all of my excuses equaled one massive rationalization to keep myself from feeling like a crushed grape? Yes. But those lame excuses had also allowed me to enjoy the evening for what it was—or had been, before Justin bolted.

But I had really started to believe there was something between us, I admitted to myself now. I went over the evidence in my mind. First, Justin had decided that he wanted to wait to meet Christy. Then he had asked me to dance. *Then* he had pulled me close for a slow dance. *And closer, and closer, and closer . . .*

I could still feel the delicious tingle of his arms encircling my body. And when I rested my head against his chest, I had felt like I was dancing on top of a cloud. The image was cheesy, but it was *true*. Justin had brought out sensations in me that I had never before experienced.

And then he had left me standing all alone like a complete idiot. No explanation, no chitchat, no funny one-liner. He had simply fled. In his wake I felt like I had been punched in the gut by a heavyweight-boxing champion.

Well, he wasn't the only one who could be rude. I wasn't going to say another unnecessary word to Justin for the rest of the night. Then again, for all I knew, the night was already officially over. Maybe Justin had jumped into his car and peeled out of the parking lot in an effort to get away from me.

But he wouldn't leave before he gets to meet Christy, I reminded myself. I had accomplished my stated goal, and I had no doubt that Justin wanted to accomplish his. In fact, he was probably outside, figuring out exactly how he was going to charm Christy into falling for him. Maybe that was why he decided to wait a little longer before taking advantage of the big introduction—he had needed time to mentally prepare himself to wow her.

I was almost at the edge of the dance floor when I felt a strong hand take hold of my arm. *Justin! He's back!* My heart leaped, and an unbidden smile (which was more like a huge grin) formed on my face.

I spun around—and found myself face-to-face with a guy who was definitely *not* Justin. My heart sank, and I felt fresh tears threatening to spill over onto my cheeks.

Luckily the guy seemed oblivious to my distress. "Hey, you're Nicole, right?" he asked.

"Yes." Great. Justin had probably given this guy a message for me. *Something polite about how he enjoyed the evening but was suddenly called home to watch a rerun of* Saturday Night Live. "Who are you?"

He smiled. "I'm Doug McGraff," he introduced himself. "We had biology together sophomore year."

"Oh . . . right." I didn't want to be a jerk, but I

wasn't in the mood to reminisce about frog dissection.

"So, do you want to dance?" he asked.

It was the last thing I had expected to come out of his mouth. For a moment I didn't know what to say. Then I took in Doug McGraff's appearance. Over six feet tall, with curly blond hair and bright blue eyes, the guy definitely fell into the hottie category.

I shrugged. "Why not?" Just because Justin didn't realize what a catch I was didn't mean that nobody else had good taste.

Another slow-dance number—something by Celine Dion—was playing. Doug put his arms around me and guided me toward the center of the dance floor. Who knew? Maybe this guy had an alias. Doug McGraff: aka Prince Charming.

"Where's your date?" I asked Doug. If we were going to be dancing cheek to cheek, we might as well get some kind of rapport going.

"I came alone," he explained. "I haven't been dating anyone in particular, so I decided to take my chances that other people's dates wouldn't go as well as they had expected." He gave me a warm smile. "And right about now, I'm thinking I made the right call. I can't think of anyone I'd rather be dancing with than you."

"Thank you," I said, feeling genuinely flattered for the first time in a long time. Doug was turning out to be just the right prescription for my heartache.

As we continued to dance, I forced all thoughts

of Justin out of my brain. *Carpe diem,* I ordered myself. Seize the day. Doug was the guy that was here, and he was the one who deserved my full attention. Unfortunately, I couldn't think of anything else to say to him.

Suddenly I felt Doug's hot breath in my ear. "You know what would look good on you?" he whispered.

Well, it wasn't a traditional icebreaker, but what the hey. "What?" I asked, tilting back my head to look into his sky blue eyes.

"Me," he answered.

Eeew. It took a moment for me to realize just how disgusting and inappropriate a come-on line that was. *Now I know the* real *reason the guy doesn't have a date,* I thought.

"You know what would look good on *you?*" I retorted.

He grinned, obviously not getting the fact that I wasn't digging his brand of wit. "Tell me," he said smugly. "What would look good on me?"

I stepped away from Doug and dropped my arms. "A glass of punch," I informed him. "Unfortunately, I don't have one at the moment— which is why I'm going to leave you standing here while I head for the refreshment table."

I strode away, wishing that Justin had been around to hear my snappy comeback. He would have gotten a kick out of it. *Not that it matters,* I reminded myself.

So much for Prince Charming. Doug had

turned out to be a lower form of life than those frogs we had dissected in biology class. The guy had turned out to be as big a jerk as the rest of the ones I had encountered during my four years of high school. Big surprise!

This evening has gone from great to bad to worse in the space of fifteen minutes, I thought. It was time to put myself out of my misery. Who wanted to spend another two hours circulating the gym, looking for moron after moron to dance with?

I wanted to cut my losses and get home as quickly as possible. If Rose and Madison noticed that I had been ditched by my so-called date, they would have fresh ammunition with which to torture me. *Now* that *would be the perfect end to a perfect evening,* I thought dismally.

I scanned the dance floor, searching for a sign of Christy. I wanted to introduce Justin to my friend and get this whole thing over with. As far as I was concerned, the clock had struck midnight, and I had turned back into a pumpkin.

"Christy, where *are* you?" I wondered aloud. I hadn't talked to her once since I had arrived at the prom—she was like a phantom tonight.

I continued across the winter wonderland of a gym, keeping my eyes peeled for either of my two best friends. Christy, apparently, was hiding in some dark corner. But I spotted Jane and Max next to the stage the band had set up. They weren't even making a show of dancing. They were simply standing in one place and making out, seemingly unaware that they were surrounded by hundreds of people.

"Sorry to interrupt, Janie," I murmured under my breath. "But I'm getting desperate."

I walked up to Jane and Max, then tapped Jane lightly on the shoulder. When she went right on smooching Max, I tapped again—harder this time.

Finally Jane turned around. "Hey, Nic!" She peered over my shoulder. "Where's Justin?"

"He's either in the parking lot, the bathroom, or halfway home," I informed her. "But assuming he's still somewhere in the vicinity, I need to find Christy. It's an emergency."

"Sorry, I saw Christy leave a few minutes ago," Jane responded, her eyes filled with empathy.

I groaned. Wonderful! Now what was I supposed to do?

Fourteen

Justin

SITTING ON THE empty bleachers beside the
Union High football field, I looked out into
the dark night and tried to clear my head of all neg-
ative thoughts. I focused on the sound of crickets
chirping, the distant hum of laughter, the bright
stars in the inky black sky.

But I have *to think about bad stuff,* I told myself. It
was imperative that I remember all of the totally
sane reasons why I didn't want to get involved with
another girl. Otherwise . . . I didn't want to think
about otherwise.

Besides, I didn't even know how Nicole felt
about me. True, I had felt some definite chemistry
when we had been dancing. And I had made her
laugh approximately thirteen times over the course
of the evening (not that I was counting). Then

there was that misty, soulful look in her eyes when I had caught her gaze over chocolate mousse at La Serenara. . . .

"Stop it!" I ordered myself aloud. "Stop thinking about Nicole like that."

Instead I pictured Laurie Swanson, the first—and only—girl I had ever fallen in love with. She was petite, with short, short hair and chocolate brown skin. And when she had looked at me with her almond-shaped eyes, I had felt like I was melting into a huge puddle of butter. I blinked at the image. Thinking of my ex-girlfriend was painful, but necessary.

I had met Laurie the first day of our freshman year at Jefferson High. I had come to Jefferson from JFK Junior High, and Laurie had come from North Junior High. We had accidentally been assigned the same locker, and the moment our hands had met at the dial of the combination lock, I had fallen deeply, irrevocably in love.

Or so I had thought. I had learned the hard way that love didn't last forever. If Laurie had *ever* loved me. She had certainly *acted* like she had. But maybe that's all it had been—an Oscar-worthy performance. And I had been the straight man, believing every word she uttered, like the fool that I was.

But the two years Laurie and I were together had been wonderful. We were inseparable, the kind of couple people referred to as JustinandLaurie, as if we were one person. There had been movies, study dates, walks in the park. We had eaten lunch together every day in the cafeteria, and we had even arranged our school schedules so that we could have as many classes together as possible.

Back then, I had been a different person. The Justin Banks people knew *before* had been outgoing, social, funny. I had been the first guy to suggest throwing a huge Halloween party and the last one to view the world through a lens of cynicism or pessimism.

Everything in my life had started to fall apart the day I was told that my mom was sick—*really* sick. She had been diagnosed with breast cancer, and doctors immediately ordered a mastectomy and a powerful course of chemotherapy. The news had been more devastating than anything I ever could have imagined, and I turned immediately to Laurie for the love and support I needed to get through every day of watching my mother suffer.

At first Laurie had been there for me. She had held my hand, hugged me, even allowed me to cry bitter tears on her shoulder. She had been the one person in the world with whom I had shared the extent of my pain. With everyone else I kept up a brave front. Mom was dealing with enough, and I had wanted to stay strong for Dad and Star.

And then, so slowly at first that I hadn't even noticed, Laurie started to pull away. She avoided coming over to our house, and our time together dwindled to the point that I would go a whole weekend without hearing from her.

On the morning that we checked my mom into

the hospital, I had shown up unannounced at Laurie's door, hoping to escape from the sadness that had become my life for just a few hours. But Laurie hadn't been happy to see me.

The moment I had looked into her eyes, I had felt cold all over. Laurie had asked me to come inside, then invited me to sit down on the sofa in her family's formal living room rather than in the den where we usually hung out for hours on end. She had perched at the edge of a Victorian-style ottoman, and she had looked like she was sitting in the dentist's office, waiting to go in for a root canal.

In her sweet, melodious voice Laurie had told me that she thought it would be better if we were just friends. She said she needed time and space to "find herself." But I had known the *real* reason for the breakup. Cancer. She didn't want to deal with the pressures of having a boyfriend with a sick mother. And worse, she didn't want to have to cope with the inevitable end of that illness.

As the memories washed over me, I stood up and made my way down the bleachers. If I was going to think about this stuff, I needed to be on the move. Otherwise I might just hang my head and sob. I headed back toward the parking lot, focusing on putting one foot in front of the other as I remembered those dark months.

I had left Laurie's house that day for the last time, feeling like my entire world had been turned upside down. Until that moment I think I had held out hope that somehow, some way Mom would pull through. But everything came crashing down around me as I realized that life wasn't the rosy prospect I had always believed it to be. Girlfriends broke hearts . . . and mothers . . . died.

From that day on, life had become a downward spiral. Mom's health had deteriorated day by day until the last flicker of hope that she would recover was extinguished. Aside from the bright moments I spent laughing with my mother at her bedside, I was engulfed in sadness.

Sam had tried to help, but I hadn't been able to let him get close. I wasn't used to talking to other guys about something so emotionally devastating. Talking about basketball and watching *Star Trek* reruns was a lot different from confessing one's deepest fears about the future. Letting go in front of Sam simply hadn't been in my nature—at least, not back then.

When my mom died at the end of a long stay in the hospital, I felt completely and utterly alone. I had felt like I was a robot going through the motions of life without connecting to anyone or anything. Laurie had shown up at my mom's funeral, but the words we had exchanged had been awkward and distant. If anything, seeing Laurie that day made me feel even worse than I already had.

In the weeks that followed my mother's death, I had resolved to myself that I would never trust and depend on another girl the way I had Laurie. Never let another girl get under my skin. I reserved my love for my dad and Star, the two people in the world who needed me the most.

And for over a year I had avoided any romantic situation with a ten-foot pole. And so far, my plan had worked. But tonight I couldn't help wondering . . . was it possible that Nicole was different?

Nicole was so *real,* so open, so honest. I couldn't imagine her acting the way Laurie had, no matter what tough situation she was confronted with. Then again, a vow was a vow. . . .

My thoughts stopped midstream as I noticed a girl rushing out of the door of the gymnasium. I was still halfway across the parking lot, but I recognized Christy immediately. Something instinctive made me quicken my pace. I jogged toward prom central, keeping my eyes glued on Christy's advancing figure.

As I got closer, I saw that tears were running down Christy's cheeks, and her skin was so pale that she looked almost like a ghost. *Now,* I thought. *Now is the time to talk to her.*

I rushed forward. "Christy?" I called out.

She stopped. "Hey . . . Justin, right?" She was drying her eyes as she spoke and clearly attempting a weak smile.

"Right." I paused, not knowing exactly how to proceed. "Do you, uh, want to tell me what's wrong?" I asked hesitantly.

"Nothing's wrong," she responded, her voice overly bright. "Everything is just fine."

I knew she was lying. And I was fairly sure that she knew I knew she was lying. What she didn't know—or at least remember at the moment—was that I understood what she was going through.

Despite the long, black, strapless dress and strappy high heels, Christy looked like a lost child. My heart went out to her, just as it had the day I had spotted her in Claire's Boutique.

"Christy, you and I have actually met once before," I explained. "Well, not officially, but your face has stuck with me ever since."

I had to talk to her. With every passing moment I was more sure that Christy's tears were related to her mother's illness. And it was imperative that I reach out . . . that I try to lend my support in any way I could.

She looked confused. "We met? Where? At the mall?"

I shook my head. "No, at the hospital. We were both in the waiting room of the cancer ward. My mom was sick too."

"Oh," she responded softly, recognition slowly dawning in her eyes. "Right."

"Are you crying because of your mom?" I asked gently. "You can tell me. Really."

"Yes," Christy whispered. The tears began to flow again, and she pulled a rumpled Kleenex from her tiny silk purse.

"Is it bad?" I asked. "Has she gotten worse?"

Christy nodded, dabbing her eyes with the Kleenex. "I appreciate your concern, Justin. I really do."

"But . . . ?" I asked.

"But please don't tell anyone that you saw me—especially that you saw me crying. I know my friends care about me, but I'm not ready to share my feelings." She took a deep, steadying breath. "I don't want anyone's pity. I just can't handle that right now."

"I won't tell the others," I promised without hesitation. "You can trust me."

I knew from personal experience that each person handled something like a parent's illness in his or her own way. It wasn't my place to tell Christy what she did or didn't need. All I could do was let her know that she wasn't alone.

"Thanks, Justin," she responded. "I just . . ."

"You don't have to explain," I assured her. "Remember, I've been there."

"Your mom . . . didn't make it?" she asked. But I could see in her eyes that she already knew the answer to that question.

"No, she died last year," I told Christy, feeling the same deep ache I felt every time I said that sentence out loud.

"I'm so sorry, Justin—"

"I'm okay," I interrupted, not wanting to put Christy in the position of having to comfort *me* at a time like this. "It gets easier to deal with every day."

She nodded mutely. "Well, I had better go . . . but thanks for talking to me. It helped."

I took the stub of my prom ticket out of the inside pocket of my tuxedo and handed it to Christy. I had written my phone number on the back of it earlier in the evening before I had realized that pushing myself on her when she was having a good time wasn't such a bright idea.

"Promise that you'll call me if you ever want to talk," I said to Christy. "I really do know what you're going through."

Christy smiled. A real smile this time. "I just might take you up on that, Justin."

I watched as she turned and headed across the parking lot. Well, I had done it. I had met Christy and offered her my support. There was nothing more I could do, at least not right now.

I walked toward the door of the gymnasium. Now that I had faced some of my demons, it was time to go back inside and find Nicole. She was either having a great time dancing with some other guy—or she was mad that I had stranded her on the dance floor. Or both.

Just as I was about to enter the prom, none other than Nicole herself walked out of the gym. "Hey," I greeted her. "I was just about to come inside and find you."

She raised her eyebrows. "I wasn't sure you were still on the premises," she said icily.

Oops. She *was* mad. "Listen, I didn't mean to rush off like that," I apologized. "I just needed to get some air."

She held up one hand to silence me. "Don't worry about it, Justin."

"Okay—"

"Here's the thing," she interrupted. "It's over. The night is a failure."

Fifteen

Nicole

I STARED AT Justin, my hands on my hips, and waited for him to respond to my statement that the night was a categorical flop. But he didn't say anything. Justin was just looking at me like I was crazy.

"Why is the night a failure?" he asked finally. "What happened?"

Justin was so mellow, so sweet, looking at me with real concern. It was hard to ignore the feelings that had been stirring inside me all evening. *Remember that you're mad at him,* I ordered myself.

"Christy left the prom already," I explained. "I went to find her, and Jane said she left a few minutes ago." Justin didn't look particularly disappointed. Maybe he didn't get what I was saying. "So I can't introduce you to her tonight," I said, spelling out the problem. "I can't hold up my end of the bargain."

"Oh, well," Justin responded mildly. *"C'est la vie."*

Jeez. Justin was one surprise after another. The guy who had flat out refused to go to the prom with me—until I had promised him a chance with my friend—now seemed totally unperturbed by the fact that he had wasted his time.

Don't read anything into this, I told myself. *He's just being nice.* Justin wasn't the type to throw a tantrum or do anything that resembled rudeness (aside, of course, from leaving me in the middle of the dance floor for no apparent reason).

"We can go now," I announced. "You've done more than your part tonight."

Justin was silent for a moment, then he grinned. "Why don't we hang out for a while longer?" he suggested. "The band is playing good music. We could take another stab at dancing."

"I don't know. . . ." Justin was an enigma—one I doubted I would ever fully understand. *Not that I'll have the chance.* Cold, hot, warm, cool, hot, cold. I never knew exactly where he was coming from.

"Come on, Nicole," he urged. "It would be a shame to waste our finery when there's still so much of the night left."

Time seemed suspended as I considered what Justin had said. There was a big part of me that wanted to leave the prom this very minute. The less time I spent with Justin, the better. I knew, deep inside, that the more hours I passed in his company, the more I would fall for him. And I didn't want to step knowingly into a minefield of disappointment. Not when I was this close to finishing my senior year without the complication of having fallen for the wrong guy.

But there was another voice inside me. The one that had made me track down Justin and beg him to go to the prom with me. Sure, I had pledged to avoid social ruin by bringing the hottest guy I had ever seen to the dance. But it wasn't as if I were the kind of person who would lose sleep over a couple of members of the Witch Brigade making fun of me. There had been some essential part of my being that had *needed* to go to the prom.

There was also some essential part of my being that found the prospect of spending another few hours with Justin totally and completely irresistible. The guy of my dreams was standing right in front of me, and I wanted to be with him more than anything else in the world. *Hey, we'll always have the prom,* I thought, already resigning myself to the heartache that would inevitably follow this evening.

"Okay," I agreed at last. "Let's stay."

Justin smiled and held out his arm for me to take. "Madam, your chariot awaits."

I took his arm, unable to resist the urge to laugh. I was Cinderella again, back at the ball. Now all I needed was a real-life fairy godmother to sprinkle me with magic dust and tell me that I was going to get everything I wanted.

*   *   *

Two hours later my feet were in considerably worse condition, but my mood had improved by about a hundred times. Justin and I had danced together to a dozen pounding rock tunes, laughing, twirling, and shaking like all of the other couples at the prom. At one point we had even formed an impromptu (and ridiculous-looking) conga line with Max and Jane.

A few weeks ago I wouldn't have believed that I could have so much fun engaging in such stereotypically teenage activities. Now I couldn't imagine having stayed home or having passed the night building up my meager savings with a baby-sitting job. Whatever I had spent (and I shuddered when I thought of the total dollar amount) was more than worth it. Tonight a whole new side of Nicole Gilmore had decided to stand up and be counted.

"If I drink one more glass of this punch, my blood-sugar level is going to be too high for me to drive legally," Justin commented.

"Maybe we can find a cup of coffee and try to bring you down," I suggested.

We were standing near the refreshment table (which was now strewn with crushed paper cups and cookie crumbs), taking a break from dancing. The crowd had thinned out, and the floor was littered with bedraggled decorations.

Justin ladled himself another glass of the neon pink punch. "Then again, I like to live dangerously."

I smiled, trying in vain to ignore all of the subtle (and not so subtle) signs that the prom was almost over. I wished it would go on forever so that I wouldn't have to say good night—and good-bye—to Justin.

"Ladies and gentlemen, you've been a great audience," the band leader announced from the stage. "We've got one more tune for you. Pair up and cuddle up—it's gonna be a slow one."

Pair. Cuddle. Slow. Those key words echoed through my brain, and my heart started to pound. Justin and I hadn't danced to any ballads since he had come back inside. And I wasn't about to put my dignity on the line by asking him to dance to this one. If he said no, I wouldn't be able to handle it.

My heart actually skipped a beat as I watched him set down his full cup of punch on the table. My mouth was so dry that I wasn't sure I would be able to speak when Justin turned to me.

"May I have the last dance?" he asked, his gaze so intense that I felt like he was looking straight into my soul.

"Uh, yeah. I mean, yes, of course. Prom wouldn't be prom without the infamous last dance."

Justin took my hand and led me into the middle of what was left of the crowd. Once again we were face-to-face under the disco ball. Hopefully Justin wouldn't bolt in the middle of the song this time.

He placed a hand on each side of my waist and pulled me close. "I'm glad it's a slow one," he said softly. "I was, um, getting pretty tired."

"Same here," I responded. But the fact that I

131

was happy about the tune being a ballad had nothing to do with being tired.

As we started to move to the music, small shivers traveled up and down my spine. I never knew that a guy's hands could feel so good. Justin's fingers brushed against the soft, tender skin on the underside of my wrist, and I felt a tingle that was more like the spark of a firecracker.

I can't breathe, I thought. *Yes, I can. No, I can't.* I struggled to focus on the music and the other couples on the dance floor. Anything to distract me from the tantalizing feel of Justin's arms around me.

"I guess there's a reason why people get so excited about the prom," Justin said. "Until tonight I couldn't understand why anyone would want to subject themselves to this kind of thing."

"I know what you mean," I answered. Did that mean Justin was glad he came along, despite the fact that he hadn't actually gotten to meet Christy? "I'm glad Rose and Madison acted the way they did. Otherwise I would have stayed home tonight."

I couldn't believe I had just admitted that. I wasn't one of those girls that babbled every thought that came into her head. And I'd had no intention of telling Justin that the night had come to mean more than a dare to me. But . . . well, looking into his eyes, it was hard not to be totally honest.

A companionable silence fell between us. For some amount of time that was either less than a minute or forever, we simply swayed to the soft sounds of the music. I sighed contentedly, wishing I could fall asleep right here in Justin's warm, safe arms.

Justin cleared his throat. "Nicole, I really want to thank you," he said. "I haven't had an evening like this in a long time."

Okay, *now* I couldn't breathe. For real. Or speak. I wasn't even sure if my ears were working right. I must have imagined the husky tone in Justin's voice.

"I, uh, you're welcome." I could have shut my mouth and let it go at that. But I was compelled to press on. "What do you mean?"

He didn't answer right away, and I thought that perhaps I had just thought those last words rather than speaking them out loud. "It's just . . . well, I forgot how much fun it is to dance and laugh and . . . just hang out with somebody besides my friend Sam."

I closed my eyes. I hadn't been imagining the husky tone in his voice. I had heard it again, and this time I was positive. *Please, let him be talking to me the way a guy talks to a girl he's really into,* I pleaded with the universe.

But I couldn't let down my defenses. I wasn't going to fall into that trap. Especially since I had spent the last several hours convincing myself that I could say good-bye to Justin without regrets. If I started to believe that there was the tiniest possibility that he had feelings for me . . . it would all be over.

"I'm sorry you didn't get more face time with

Christy," I said tentatively. "I know that's the only reason you agreed to come tonight."

I held my breath, praying with every fiber of my being that Justin would lean forward and whisper in my ear that he didn't care if he *ever* met Christy. I wanted him to take my face in his hands and kiss me, right here under the disco ball. *I don't even care if Rose and Madison are watching,* I thought. *This kiss would be for me and me alone.*

Justin shrugged (as well as he could with my arms wrapped around his neck). "Don't worry about it," he said easily. "I'll catch up with Christy another time. I'm sure of it."

I exhaled, and as the breath left my lungs, so did all of the good feelings I had been storing inside myself for the last few hours. That was that. I didn't need to hear anything else to know that nothing had changed between the time I had approached Justin yesterday afternoon and now.

Okay, one thing had changed. I was no longer just the bizarre stranger who had accosted Justin outside his high school. Now I was something of a buddy, a pal, a *compadre*. Maybe Justin would want to hang out and watch a baseball game together or share a basket of cheese fries at the food court in the mall. Or, even worse, maybe Justin would want to double date. He and Christy, and me and some nameless, faceless jerk.

But he hasn't forgotten about Christy. Not for a second. My heart was in the soles of my feet as the band finished the song. As soon as the last strum of the guitar faded into silence, the blaring lights of the gymnasium came up.

The winter wonderland was gone. In its place was a colossal mess. Even the disco ball now seemed totally out of whack with the rest of the gym. Couples were streaming out of the prom as chaperons walked around and picked up empty cups and discarded paper plates.

The fairy tale was officially over. I felt my face getting hot, and there was a tremendous squeezing sensation in my chest. Oh no! I knew what was coming. Any moment now tears would start to run down my cheeks.

"I'll meet you outside," I told Justin, my voice barely more than a squeak. I couldn't just stand there like my heart hadn't been flattened into a crepe. I had to get away from Justin.

Before Justin had a chance to say anything, I turned and raced across the floor of the gymnasium. I was too proud to run, so I executed a sort of race walk that I'd seen middle-aged women in my neighborhood doing every morning.

Don't cry, I ordered myself. *Not now.* But as I continued to speed across the floor, one tear and then another slid down my face. I couldn't help it. This level of misery couldn't be contained within a pair of dry eyes.

I broke out of the fast walk and began to run. But as I neared the door of the gym, I tripped on the hem of my long, stupid dress. "Ouch!" I yelped, falling to my knees.

I stood up quickly, hoping no one had seen me. But as I started to move again, I realized that something was wrong. My legs weren't working quite right. I lifted the hem of my dress and looked down. Perfect! The heel of one of my shoes had broken off.

Gwen is going to kill me, I thought. This was her favorite pair of shoes. But I didn't stop to look for the missing heel. I couldn't. I had to get out to the parking lot as quickly as possible—and as far ahead of Justin as possible.

I needed at least a minute alone to pull myself together before Justin drove me home. I was upset enough as it was. I didn't need the added humiliation of having Justin see me so emotional.

At last I reached the parking lot. The air had cooled, but it was still a beautiful night. I slipped off both of my shoes and walked slowly toward the car, catching my breath as I swung the ruined heels at my side.

I inhaled deeply, willing myself to find that calm, distant room in my head. The one that was safe and closed and protected from the outside world. *You're all right, Nicole,* I told myself. *You don't need anyone.*

I took one last deep breath. I had gone from deep depression to a sort of numbness. At least for now. But all I needed was to get through the next twenty minutes. Once I got home, I would be free to sob into my pillow until I turned thirty.

It was strange. I had thought tonight was all about the Witch Brigade and their evil attitude. But it had turned out that the night had been about me . . . and the fact that I was fundamentally unlovable.

Sixteen

Justin

I FOUND NICOLE in the parking lot, waiting by the side of my car. She didn't exactly light up when she saw me coming.

"Hey," I greeted her. "Why did you rush off?"

She shrugged. "I was ready to get out of there. Once the lights came up, the place looked like a winter *wasteland*. It was depressing."

Okay. Apparently Nicole didn't like bright lights. Or maybe she wasn't being totally honest. There was always the possibility that Nicole had been afraid that one of the chaperons was going to recruit her to help clean up the totally trashed gymnasium. More than one of them had suggested to me on my way out that I could stay for the "cleanup party."

"Well, Max and Jane asked us to wait a few

137

minutes before we take off," I informed her. "Jane wanted to say good-bye to you."

Nicole opened the passenger-side door of the car. "Jane can call me tomorrow. I'm tired."

All righty, then, I thought, unnerved by Nicole's 180-degree change of attitude. Had I done something wrong? Or did Nicole magically turn into a shrew when the clock struck midnight?

I slid into the driver's seat and started the car. I had been planning to ask Nicole if she would let me take her out for a late-night cup of coffee, but clearly that was a bad plan. She wasn't hiding the fact that she wanted to rid herself of my company ASAP.

"Thanks again for tonight," I said pleasantly, hoping her bad mood was a passing phenomenon. "I had fun." I pulled out of the parking lot and started toward the Gilmores' house.

Nicole sighed deeply, settling into her seat. "I broke one of my heels," she announced. "But it's not *my* heel. It's my sister, Gwen's, heel."

"That's too bad." I switched on the radio and turned the dial, searching for a station playing some kind of soothing, classical music. "Maybe you can get it fixed."

She shook her head. "I *can't* get it fixed because I lost the stupid heel. Okay?"

"Okay." Man. This girl had some serious personality issues. One would have thought that *I* had broken her shoe.

Nicole sighed again—this time it was sort of a

resigned, tired, I-know-I-was-just-really-rude-but-I-don't-want-to-say-I'm-sorry kind of a sigh. "Listen, Justin, I appreciate your concern. But there's nothing you can do, so why don't we just drop it?"

"Good idea." I didn't have much to say on the subject of women's shoes anyway. Nor was I much good at coaxing girls out of a weird state of mind.

Nicole closed her eyes, and the conversation was officially over. Just like the prom. I stared straight ahead at the road, trying to figure out what was going on. Nicole just didn't seem like the sort of person whose life fell apart over a broken heel. And from what she had said about her sister during dinner, I doubted that Gwen was really going to give her that hard a time about it.

So what is it? I asked myself. I was in a state of utter confusion, and I had no idea how I was supposed to wade through that confusion to figure out what was going on. I glanced over at Nicole. Her eyes were still closed, and she looked a million miles away.

I shouldn't even be wasting my time thinking about this, I realized. It wasn't as if I wanted to go out with Nicole. Her bad mood simply wasn't my problem to cope with. She could be a grouch for the rest of her life—it meant nothing to me.

After what seemed like the longest ride since man first flew to the moon, I finally turned onto Nicole's street. "Wake up, sleepyhead," I said. "We're almost there."

She opened her eyes but didn't bother to respond.

I pulled up in front of the Gilmores' house and turned off the car so that I could walk Nicole to the door. But before I even had the chance to undo my seat belt, Nicole had opened her car door and jumped out.

"Wait!" I called. But Nicole was already heading toward the front path that led to her front door. "I guess you don't want me to walk you to the door," I said softly.

What if her parents are watching from the window? I thought. *They'll think I'm the rudest date in history.*

I didn't want to care. But I did. Nicole's attitude hurt. I had thought we were becoming friends, but she obviously didn't agree. I got out of the car anyway, determined to say a proper good night. Maybe Nicole was comfortable ignoring the niceties—but I wasn't.

By the time I started up the front path, she was already sliding her key into the lock of the front door. "Thanks again, Justin," she called.

"You're welcome," I called back. "But I'm the one who should be thanking you."

The door opened, and Nicole slipped into the house. So much for attempting the niceties. I stopped in my tracks. As I was about to turn back to the car, Nicole stuck her head out of the doorway.

"And I really am sorry I didn't get you your big date with Christy!" she added.

A date? I had never wanted a *date* with Christy. I just wanted to offer her an ear. Obviously Nicole had misunderstood my intentions.

"Nicole, I—"

"Good night," she interrupted. A moment later the door slammed shut.

Well, that's that. Good-bye, prom. Good-bye, Nicole. This morning I had wanted nothing more than for this evening to come to a merciful end. Now I felt totally deflated.

And sad. Nicole Gilmore had disappeared from my life as quickly as she had entered it. Absurdly, I felt like a part of me had vanished too.

"Juuuustinnn!" Star's voice penetrated my unconscious, and I pried open my eyes. Light was streaming in through the window, and the clock beside my bed read 9:12 A.M. "Justtttiiiiin!"

I had been having a dream. Something about circus elephants and house cats wearing prom dresses and broken high-heeled shoes. *I'm getting weirder as I get older,* I noted.

And then it all came back to me. The prom. Nicole. Meeting Christy. Nicole basically refusing to speak to me in the car on the way home. The whole night ran through my mind on ultra-fast-forward in vivid Technicolor.

"I'll be down in a minute!" I shouted to Star. Since Mom died, we had made a habit of fixing a big Sunday morning breakfast together every week.

Now I know why I'm so tired and groggy, I thought. I had lain awake most of the night, going over every detail of the night in my head. I had tried everything to fall asleep—counting sheep, pacing the floor, even drinking a little warm milk (which was disgusting). But every time I closed my eyes, another image from the evening would pop into my head.

I pulled on a pair of sweatpants and one of my softest, oldest T-shirts. I was going to eat breakfast, read the paper, maybe go for a jog. Once I got back into my routine, I would forget all about the whirlwind of emotions I had experienced last night. My strange, early morning dreams had been my way of putting a period at the end of the whole event. I had been expunging all extraneous memories from my subconscious.

Walking out of my room, I inhaled deeply, absorbing the aroma of pancakes emanating from the kitchen. Great! A stack of pancakes topped with Star's special peanut-butter-and-banana spread was exactly what I needed to dissipate that nagging feeling of disappointment that was refusing to go away.

"It's about time," Star said the moment I walked into the kitchen. "Did you stay out all night or something?"

"*Nooo,*" I responded. "I just wanted to sleep in for a while. Sue me."

Star raised her eyebrows with the kind of avidly curious expression that only a sixth-grade girl can muster. "I thought you would be in a better mood after your big date!"

"Who said I'm in a bad mood?" I asked, taking over at the griddle. "It's a beautiful morning. Hey, where's Dad, anyway?"

And if you want to know about bad moods, talk to Nicole, I added silently. I flipped a couple of pancakes, then slid them onto a plate. Star took the plate and went to work with the peanut butter and bananas.

"He went to get a newspaper," she explained. So?" she added, spreading the peanut butter an inch thick. "How was the prom? Are you in love?"

I laughed. "In love? Of course not!"

Star added some bananas to her creation. "Well, do you at least *like* her?" she asked.

I thought for a moment. Of course, I *liked* Nicole. Aside from the fact that she had decided she hated me at the end of the night, she was the perfect girl.

"Yes, I like her," I said finally. "She's a great person."

I only had to look into Star's eyes for a split second to know that she was far from done with the game of twenty questions. She had probably spent most of last night composing a list of everything she wanted to know about my experience at the Union High senior prom.

Might as well give her the breakdown of the entire evening, I thought. I would never get out of this kitchen otherwise.

"We had an awesome time," I declared. "Nicole took me to this really fancy restaurant. We ate snails and made fun of the waiters, and Nicole pretended for a while that she didn't speak English."

I laughed at the memory. The girl was nuts! I

could still see the confused look on the busboy's face when Nicole tried to ask him for another glass of water in a made-up language. Star started to laugh too.

"She sounds funny," Star proclaimed. "I think I'd like her."

I nodded. "You would. Man, *she* could help you shop for a dress. You should have seen what she was wearing. . . . She looked beautiful."

Then again, Nicole would look beautiful in denim shorts and a ripped sweatshirt, I thought. She had the cheekbones of an Egyptian goddess.

"What about the prom itself?" Star asked. "Were the decorations nice? Did you dance? Did you meet any cool people?"

"Yeah, the Union High gym looked pretty amazing," I told her, remembering the thousands of tiny lights, the huge disco ball, and the pretty little tables. "Nicole suggested we try to start a pickup game of basketball to see if anyone would abandon the dance floor for the hoops."

"Did you slow dance?" Star pressed. "Was it romantic?"

Yes, it was romantic, I thought. But I wasn't about to tell Star what it felt like to hold Nicole in my arms. There were some things a guy needed to keep to himself. And that was definitely one of them.

"We danced," I said casually. "After all, it was the *prom.*"

"You know, for a guy who isn't in love, you're talking an awful lot about Nicole," Star commented.

"Are you guys going to go on another date?" she asked as I handed her another plate of pancakes.

I groaned. "Star, you ask way too many questions," I told her. "And for your information, no, we're *not* going out again."

But she was right. I was sort of going on and on about Nicole. But that was just because it had been so long since I'd been out with a girl. Just because I had sworn off girls didn't mean I wasn't a normal guy with normal desires. That didn't mean I had to *act* on those desires. I knew better.

"Besides, Nicole totally turned on me at the end of the night," I continued. "She would barely talk to me in the car on the way home. One second we were dancing . . . and the next thing I knew, she, like, hated me." I paused. "But who cares? It wasn't a real date."

"I don't get it." Star frowned at the jar of peanut butter. "How could going to the prom with somebody not be a *date?* That's, like, the *definition* of a date."

I shook my head. "Not in our case." I poured another ladle full of batter onto the griddle and watched tiny bubbles appear on the pancake. "You're too young to understand. Why don't you just forget it?"

Her eyes flashed, and she put her hands on her hips. I wanted to laugh. In her ice-cream-cone-patterned pajamas, my little sister was hardly threatening. But I knew that if even one giggle escaped, I would have a very angry sixth-grader on my hands.

"Why don't *you* just explain why it wasn't a real date?" she demanded. "I'm not a little kid, you know. I have *insights*."

This time I couldn't help myself. I laughed out loud. "Okay, Miss Know-it-all, I'll explain why it wasn't a *real* date," I relented.

She finished the second plate of pancakes and set them on the table. "Do you remember a girl with long brown hair from the hospital?" I asked, sitting down across from Star. "She was in the waiting room of the cancer ward a couple of times."

Star furrowed her brow. "I think so . . . but I'm not sure. It's hard to remember anything about that time except for how sick Mom was."

I nodded, and we were both quiet for a moment . . . remembering. "Well, her name is Christy, and she's a friend of Nicole's," I explained. "I recognized her at the mall that day you were on the endless hunt for the perfect dress."

"I remember," Star told me through a mouthful of pancakes.

"When Nicole asked me to the prom, I said no at first," I admitted. "But then I saw that Christy was with her, waiting by the car."

Star gulped half her glass of orange juice, then looked at me with confusion in her eyes. "So . . . you really wanted a date with Christy?"

"No! I didn't want a date with *anybody*." I couldn't believe I was discussing this stuff with my little sister. Sam would have been laughing his head off if he had been around for this conversation. "I wanted to meet Christy and offer her some help," I explained. "I mean, I know what it's like to have a sick mom—and there was something in her face. . . . I could tell that her mom wasn't doing well."

"The Look," Star said quietly. She was young, but she knew a lot about pain. Too much.

"So I told Nicole that I would go to the prom with her on one condition. She had to introduce me to Christy."

Star took another bite of her pancakes, studying my face as she chewed. Finally she swallowed. "Justin, it's obvious you have a crush on Nicole."

"I—"

"Let me talk!" she interrupted, waving her fork in my face. "As I was saying, it's *obvious* you like Nicole. A lot. And I think she likes you too."

"Star, I told you—by the end of the night Nicole was a totally different person. She was cold and distant and . . . she didn't even let me walk her to the front door of her house."

The image made me feel sad all over again. The sound of Nicole slamming the door still echoed through my head. I was never going to see her again. . . .

"Duh!" Star exclaimed, tapping me on the forehead with her sticky fork. "Nicole is obviously *so* into you. But she turned cold at the end of the night because *she* thinks *you* like *Christy*."

"Huh." I was momentarily speechless.

Was it possible that Star was right? A tiny flicker of hope ignited within my heart. What she'd said *did* make a certain amount of sense. I went over the evening again in my head. And there had been one other point at which Nicole was less than her usual charming self. It was when I had left her alone on the dance floor. She had even said that she had thought I'd gone home without her.

"Justin, she *likes* you," Star repeated. "I'm a girl. I know about this kind of thing."

Maybe Star was right. But that didn't change the fact that I had no desire for a girlfriend. Even one as awesome as Nicole.

"Nonetheless, I don't want to get involved with anyone," I told Star, repeating myself for probably the hundredth time. "So it doesn't matter."

Star pushed away her now empty plate. "Justin, you're living in the past," she announced. "I know what happened with Laurie. I'm young—but I'm not stupid."

"What does Laurie have to do with anything?" I protested. "I haven't even *mentioned* Laurie."

"I know," she responded. "But you're using your past with Laurie to keep yourself from moving into the future. A future that *doesn't* include Mom."

"Mom doesn't have anything to do with this either!" I practically shouted. "I don't want to date for my own, very sane, reasons."

Star shook her head. "This *does* have something to do with Mom," she insisted. "Her life is over, but ours *isn't.*"

"I know that," I said quietly. "I'm here; you're here. Life goes on."

"But you're *not* letting life go on," Star continued. "By not letting yourself risk getting hurt again, you're living in denial of reality." She paused. "There's always going to be the chance you could get hurt, Justin. That doesn't mean we shouldn't take chances."

I looked down at my plate. My pancakes were mostly eaten, but I couldn't even remember bringing the fork to my mouth. Star's words had gotten to me. And she was absolutely right.

If Mom's death has taught us anything, it's that life is the most precious thing there is, I thought. My mother wouldn't have wanted me to cloister myself away and stop taking chances. She would have wanted me and Star and my dad to go on without her. She would have wanted us to live the best, happiest lives we could—even without her.

And there was no doubt that I couldn't be totally alive without opening myself up to the possibility of hurt. It just wasn't possible to go through every day without feeling moments of pain, loneliness, even desperation. But it also wasn't possible to go through life without those moments of joy. And lately . . . I hadn't been feeling *anything*.

Until last night. Last night I had been on top of the world. Not just because it was fun to be at a dance or eat at a nice restaurant. I had been on cloud nine because of Nicole. She had made me feel like a real human being again.

"You're right," I said to Star. "You may be only in sixth grade, but you've got a lot of insights."

Star grinned. "At last! He sees the light!"

"You're pretty smart," I told my little sister. "You know that?"

"Yes, I know that!" she declared. "But we're not talking about my brain right now. We're talking about how you're going to convince Nicole to go on another date with you—a *real* date this time."

But I was one step ahead of her. I had already started to formulate a plan . . . one that would show Nicole that she was more than simply a "business transaction" to me. *And if it works . . . I'll be the happiest guy in the world.*

Seventeen

Nicole

BY LATE SUNDAY morning my eyeballs felt like they had been pried out and put back into their sockets with Krazy Glue. I hadn't been this tired since I had stayed up all night to watch a Nick At Nite *Wonder Years* marathon. By my best estimation, I had managed to get about two and a half hours of sleep.

I promised myself I wasn't going to lose sleep over Justin, and that's exactly what I did, I thought. I had sat up in bed, hour after hour, going over every detail of my nondate with Justin in my head.

I just didn't get it. Justin didn't even *know* Christy. How could he be so stuck on her . . . especially after the two of us had had such an awesome time together? Yes, Christy was pretty—she was beautiful. But it wasn't as if I belonged in the dog pound. Plenty of guys had let me know in crude but no uncertain terms that I was an attractive girl.

"Maybe he *didn't* have a good time," I speculated aloud. Maybe he really was just being a gentleman when he laughed at my jokes and gazed into my eyes and cut to the front of the punch line when I said I was about to faint from thirst.

I pulled on my favorite pair of faded denim overalls and a graying white tank top. I probably wouldn't put on another dress until the day of my high-school graduation. And after that . . . maybe never again.

The single white rose Justin had given me was sitting on top of my desk next to the stub of my ticket to the dance. I picked it up and breathed deeply. The smell was already fading—I hoped my memories would drift into the ether as quickly. *But I want to save the corsage,* I decided. A girl went to her senior prom only one time, and it was an event that deserved to be memorialized for posterity.

I had learned how to press flowers at Girl Scout camp in the fourth grade. My knowledge of the process was vague at best, but it would have to do. I pulled volume *A* through *O* of my *Oxford English Dictionary* off my bookshelf and set it on the desk.

I opened the enormous book and leafed through it until I reached the approximate middle. *Forwrought. Foryellow. Foryeme. Foryield. Forzando.* Too bad *failure* wasn't on this page. It would be slightly more appropriate.

"Good-bye, rose," I said, feeling like a total dork. I

rested the corsage gently between the pages, laid the ticket stub next to it, then carefully shut the huge book. Next I took the other volume of the *OED* from the bookshelf and placed it on top of the first one.

"There," I announced. "In two weeks I'll have one ticket stub and a beautiful, dead, dry flower as proof that I actually went to the prom."

In the meantime I had no desire to spend the rest of the day staring at the lavender dress hanging from my closet door. In fact, I never wanted to see it again. I crossed the room toward the closet, remembering the soft touch of the lavender silk against my legs as I had danced.

"You served me well," I told the dress, re-covering it in the pink plastic garment bag from Claire's Boutique. "But it's time for retirement."

I walked all the way into the roomy closet and hung the dress at the very back of the rack. Knowing the way things disappeared in there (Gwen called it the Bermuda Triangle of closets), I doubted the item would resurface until sometime in the year 2020. Which was fine with me.

I firmly shut the closet door, then collapsed onto my bed. That was it. I didn't have anything else to do until it was time for my 3:00 P.M. shift at the store. Neither Christy nor Jane had answered their phones earlier, and Gwen had gone camping for the weekend. I had all day to sit here and pine over what could never be.

Oh, joy! I thought sarcastically. I almost wished I hadn't finished that math assignment Friday night.

For some reason, I always found working with concrete numbers soothing. At least I didn't have to worry about seeing Rose and Madison on Monday. They would be giving me nothing but props for my totally hot date.

I sighed deeply, thinking about the prom photo that my mom had snapped the night before. When she and Dad had taken off for a day of errands this morning, she had asked if I wanted her to take the film by One Hour photo. I had said no, but now I wished I had taken her up on the offer. I was longing to see Justin's face—even if that face was two-dimensional.

Of course, looking at the picture would be mental torture. It would remind me of everything I had lost when the clock had struck midnight. For one night I had been Cinderella. *Too bad Justin isn't going to appear at my doorstep with a glass slipper—or in my case, a glass heel.*

I was still trying to figure out how to break the news to Gwen about her favorite pair of shoes. I would have offered to buy her a new pair, but I was already up to the bib of my overalls in debt. Then again, after I told Gwen the whole sob story about Justin, she'd probably be in a pretty forgiving mood. . . .

The doorbell rang. It was probably a magazine salesman. Or an ax murderer. *Either way, it'll be someone to talk to.* Who knew? Maybe the person at the door was Ed McMahon with my ten-million-dollar check from the Publishers Clearing House sweepstakes.

I took the stairs two at a time. At the front door I peered through the window to make sure my visitor didn't have horns or big, spiky teeth. My jaw dropped open when I saw who was standing on the front steps.

It wasn't a monster. It was Justin Banks.

My first thought was that I must have left something in his car. My second thought was that he had shown up to demand that I take him over to Christy's house for an introduction. My third thought was that I must be hallucinating.

I opened the door. This wasn't a mirage—Justin stood before me, looking as gorgeous as ever in jeans and an old T-shirt. "Justin!" I said as soon as I found my voice. "This is, uh, a surprise." *One that's making my heart beat like there was a hummingbird in my chest,* I added silently. "Did you forget something? I mean, did I forget something?"

He smiled and held out his left hand, which had been hiding behind his back. "I found this," he announced. "And I believe it belongs to you."

I stared at Justin's palm, trying to decipher what the object in his hand was. It was silver and about four inches long and looked like it would be a perfect eye-gouging tool. Finally it clicked.

"My heel!" I exclaimed. "I mean, Gwen's heel!" I grinned as I took it from Justin's outstretched hand. "Where did you *find* it?"

Justin looked down for a moment, then gave me a sort of tentative smile. "Uh . . . in a trash can outside Alta Vista," he explained.

I looked at the heel, and then I looked at Justin. Wow. He found it in a garbage can. Which meant that he had gotten up this morning and driven back to school and dug through trash for who knew how long.

"It must have taken forever to find this," I said, not knowing quite what to make of his actions. "Thanks a lot."

I was truly touched that Justin had gone to such lengths to find my missing heel. I was also relieved. I could get the shoe fixed before Gwen ever knew that it had been broken.

He shrugged. "I, um, knew it was important to you. I mean, I didn't want your sister to renounce you or anything."

Immediately I felt guilty. I had gone on so much about the broken heel in the car that I'd actually made Justin feel bad. And the truth was that losing the heel hadn't been a tragedy. I had just been worried in the car that if I didn't focus on something specific, I would start to cry.

"Well . . . thanks again," I said, wishing I were holding Justin's hand instead of the broken heel. "And I promise that I'll get Christy to call you."

I expected Justin to smile, wave, and disappear into the sunset. But he didn't. He just kept standing there, giving me a weird look.

"Do I have something on my face?" I asked, rubbing my nose.

He laughed. "No, your face is fine, Nic." Justin was staring into my eyes now, and I felt my knees threatening to give way. "It's more than fine. It's beautiful."

I was starting to think I was on *Candid Camera*. Had Justin Banks just told me that I was beautiful? "I—I, uh . . ." Nothing came out.

"I actually talked to Christy last night," Justin informed me, seeming not to notice that I was stammering and stuttering. "But not for the reason you think."

Okay. I had entered some parallel universe in which nothing I had previously known made any sense. "Why, then?" I asked.

"It's a long story," Justin said. "And one I'll tell you about someday . . . but not right now."

Someday. He had said someday. As if we were going to see each other again. *Don't get started, Nicole,* I ordered myself. I had gone down the path of hope before, and it had led to a total dead end.

"All right. I *won't* have Christy call you," I announced. "So . . . I'll see you around."

"Since I met Christy on my own, I'd like you to fulfill your part of our bargain in another way," Justin informed me.

"You want the fifty dollars?" I asked.

Justin laughed. "No! Of course not!"

"What, then?" I was searching my brain for something I had that Justin could possibly want. But unless he had a thing for girls' clothing or old dolls, he was going to be out of luck.

"I'd like you to go to *my* prom with me next weekend," he said matter-of-factly.

"Why?" I asked, dumbfounded.

He shrugged. "Let's just say I'm trying to impress someone very special."

And then it hit me. The answer was totally obvious. Justin didn't have a crush on Christy anymore—he had said as much just now. He had feelings for someone else. Somebody he wanted to see at the Jefferson prom. And he thought (probably rightly) that he would be more attractive to this girl if he had a date on his arm. In my experience, guys did stuff like that all the time.

"If I do this for you, it means we're even, right?" I asked. "No more favors, no more conditions?"

"Right," Justin said. "But—"

"I'll do it," I interrupted. "Pick me up next Saturday at eight."

With that, I shut the door in Justin's face. I didn't want to stand there and listen to him talk about this mystery girl. And I didn't want to chat about the weather. All I wanted to do was go upstairs, climb into bed, and forget that next Saturday night I was going to have to endure a whole other evening being tortured by the fact that I was with a guy who loved someone else instead of me.

Eighteen

Nicole

"NIC? ARE YOU in there?" Gwen called, knocking softly on my bedroom door.

"Come on in!" I called back.

I was halfway inside my closet, digging for my prom dress. Now that it looked like I was going to wear it again, I didn't want the thing to turn into a wrinkled mess.

I heard the door open and close behind me. "What are you *doing?*" Gwen asked with a laugh. "I've never known you to do any voluntary spring cleaning."

"I was looking for my prom dress," I explained, backing out of the closet with the plastic-covered dress clutched in my right hand. "I put it way back on the rack so that I wouldn't have to see it again until I was sixty years old."

Gwen looked confused. "Correct me if I'm wrong, but I detect there's a story here." She glanced at the dress. "And it definitely has something to do with your big night at the prom—which, by the way, I want to hear all about."

"I don't want to talk about it," I informed her.

She snorted. "Come on, Nic. Why do you think I came home today? I've only got one tiny load of laundry with me."

I hung the dress back up on the closet door, then sort of catapulted myself onto my bed. "Dinner was awesome. Rose and Madison had to eat their words." I delivered the prom rundown in a toneless voice, as if I were a robot. "The prom was awesome. Justin and I danced for hours and had a great time. The end."

"All that sounds great," Gwen announced. "What's the problem?"

I picked up the heel Justin had brought me and held it up for Gwen's inspection. "This, for one. I broke your shoe."

Gwen took the heel. "Okay . . . that news doesn't thrill me. But it's hardly a reason to dismiss your prom as a failure. There *are* shoe repairmen in this town, Nicole."

I moaned. It seemed that Gwen wasn't going to let me off the hook gracefully. She wanted to know every ugly detail.

"Justin doesn't love me," I told her. "He barely even *likes* me."

I had already figured out why he had gone to all

160

the trouble to find the missing heel. He was afraid I wouldn't agree to go to his prom, so he wanted a little extra guilt ammunition.

"How do you know?" Gwen asked. "I mean, did he come right out and tell you that he doesn't want to see you again?"

"Not exactly," I admitted. "We're actually going to *his* prom together next weekend."

Gwen reached over and rapped my forehead. "*Hello?* This is a *good* thing."

"For a normal guy and a normal girl, yes, this would be a good thing," I agreed. "But Justin and I don't operate the regular way. The only reason he even wants me to go to the prom with him is so that he can scope out some girl that he apparently wants to ask out on a real date."

"Did he actually express that fact in words?" Gwen asked. "Or are you using ESP to deduce this information?"

I shrugged. "A little bit of both," I admitted.

Gwen was quiet for a moment. "You know what I think?" she said finally. "I think you should go to the prom with Justin as if this was a typical date between a typical guy and a typical girl. I think you should drink punch and dance and forget all about this other, theoretical girl."

"But that's not going to help anything," I insisted. "I'll just fall for Justin even harder—and be hurt that much more."

"Maybe. But maybe not." She reached out and gave me a sisterly pat on the shoulder. "I don't think you're giving yourself *or* Justin enough credit. If he has any brains at all, the guy will fall madly and deeply in love with you."

"Thanks, Gwen." I appreciated that my older sister thought I was girlfriend worthy, despite all the evidence I had seen to the contrary. If only Justin saw all of the qualities in me that Gwen did . . .

"But there is one hitch," Gwen informed me.

"What's that?" I was almost afraid to hear.

"You're going to have to get yourself a new pair of shoes," Gwen proclaimed. "I'm not loaning you mine again until you're in college."

I laughed. I wished I could be as lighthearted and carefree as my sister. But how was that really possible? The man of my dreams had just asked me to go to his prom for the sole purpose of impressing "someone very special." This wasn't exactly a banner day.

But I would take Gwen's advice. I would have a good time at the prom, simply enjoying what little time I was going to have with Justin. After all, it wasn't as if a few more dances with him were going to make me feel *worse*. My heart was already broken.

"You're in this place almost as much as I am," Claire said to me later that afternoon in the middle of my shift at the boutique. "I'm beginning to think I should retire and let you take over."

I shut the drawer of the register. "No way," I told her. "I like dresses as much as the next person, but I definitely don't have your out-and-out passion for taffeta and silk."

Still, I was actually glad that I had to work this afternoon. Hanging clothes, ringing up sales, and cleaning the supply closet were simple, concrete tasks that had effectively kept my mind off Justin (more or less) for the past three hours.

I had even managed to tell Claire about the prom without getting totally upset over the lack of romantic possibilities between Justin and myself. The rhythmic activities of work had cleared my head and allowed me to attain a state of semiserenity. Justin was just a guy—not a god. There was no logical reason why I should allow myself to fall apart because Justin didn't think I was the girl of his dreams.

"How close are you to being out of debt?" Claire asked.

I groaned. "Don't even ask."

She grinned, her green eyes twinkling. "Well, I have a surprise for you." Claire reached under the counter and pulled out a small white envelope. "It's a graduation present, but I figure I'll give it to you now."

"Thanks, Claire," I said, taking the envelope. "But you didn't have to get me anything."

"I wanted to, Nic," she assured me. "Having you around has been good for business. Not just because of your skill as a salesperson, but because practically everyone you know bought their prom dress here."

I opened the envelope. Inside there was a graduation card. There was some kind of Hallmark poem printed on it, but I didn't stop to read it. My gaze fixed on the thin, prettily decorated slip of paper that Claire had slipped into the card. This Certificate Entitles *Nicole Gilmore* to One Lavender Silk Prom Dress, Courtesy of Claire's Boutique.

Tears sprang to my eyes as I absorbed the meaning of this single piece of paper. "Claire, I can't accept this," I announced. "It's way too big a gift."

She tossed her long, curly red hair over one shoulder and arched her eyebrows. "You can and you *will* accept it," she informed me. She opened up a notebook and scanned some figures. "Now— since the dress is a gift and you've worked so many extra shifts during the last few weeks, my calculations tell me that I owe you *more* than enough to cover your prom tickets and that expensive dinner at La Serenara that you put on your credit card."

"Thank you, Claire." I felt a huge wave of relief wash over me. Financial freedom! Yeah! I put my arms around my boss and gave her a huge hug. "I can't tell you how much this means to me."

My day had gone from bad to okay to great. Now I could even buy a new pair of high heels to wear to Justin's prom—not that it really mattered what I wore.

I was still smiling when the bell over the door of the shop chimed, and Jane walked in. I noticed immediately that her eyes were red and her face looked pale.

"What's wrong?" I asked. "Did you and Max have a fight after Justin and I left last night?"

Jane shook her head. "I just found out that Christy's mom went into the hospital last night. She's not doing very well—at all."

"What?" I suddenly felt numb. I knew that Mrs. Redmond had been sick, but I had no idea that she needed to be hospitalized. Christy never wanted to talk about it.

"That's why Christy left the prom so suddenly last night," Jane explained. "She found out her mom had gone into the hospital, and she left to be with her."

"She didn't tell us . . . ," I whispered. "Why didn't she tell us?"

Jane shook her head. "I don't know, Nic. But we know now."

"Don't worry about your shift," Claire told me. "Go be with your friend."

"Thanks, Claire. Again."

I grabbed my backpack and followed Jane out of the store. Suddenly the prom and Justin and the Witch Brigade seemed like the most unimportant things on earth. Our friend was in trouble, and she needed us. *And we'll be there for her,* I thought. *No matter what happens.*

Nineteen

Justin

SITTING ACROSS THE table from Nicole at Pete's Lobster House on Saturday night, I could hardly believe this was the same girl I had accompanied to her senior prom just a week ago. Nicole was being nice enough, but she hadn't made one joke about wagging lobster tails or filling squirt guns with the butter sauce.

Nicole looks beautiful, but she seems tired, I thought. *Tired and sad.* For the first time in a long time, I realized that I felt . . . well, like someone's boyfriend. Not that Nicole had done anything to make me feel like I deserved that title. When I had called her during the week, she hadn't been any more effusive than she had been last Sunday when I was standing on her stoop.

I was beginning to accept the fact that Star had

been wrong. Nicole didn't like me at all. She hadn't wanted to go on a real date with me, and she *hadn't* cared that in her mind I had only agreed to go to her prom because I had a crush on Christy. Still . . . now that I had opened my heart, it was hard to close it. I had to try to get through to her.

"Nicole, do you want to talk about what's bothering you?" I asked. "I mean, you can't be frowning like that just because I'm taking up your Saturday night—unless you were dying to watch the *Mary Tyler Moore* marathon on Nick At Nite."

She shook her head and gave me a small smile. "Nah . . . I don't want to bring you down right before the prom. You need to be at your best to impress that special someone."

Special someone? Suddenly the words I had spoken to Nicole last Sunday echoed through my mind. She had thought I was talking about someone *else*. So maybe there was still hope. Maybe I still had a chance!

But there was something I needed to do. I needed to tell Nicole the whole truth. I had to tell her about my mom, and Laurie, and the real reason I had wanted to meet Christy. Otherwise she was never going to understand why I had been so hot and cold . . . why even though I had wanted to more than anything else in the world, I hadn't let my defenses down enough to kiss her on the dance floor when I'd had the chance.

"Nicole, there's something I need to tell you," I said softly.

She looked up from her lobster. "What is it?" she asked. "Something about how I'm supposed to act when we see the special someone?"

"No," I said firmly, shaking my head. "I need to explain the real reason that I asked you to introduce me to Christy—the reason that that was my condition when you invited me to your prom."

As soon as I finished speaking, I saw that tears had started to well in Nicole's eyes. One escaped and slid down her cheek, and she raised her hand to brush it away. The truth began to dawn on me, but I was almost afraid to ask.

"It's Christy's mom, isn't it?" I asked, before Nicole had a chance to say anything. "She's getting even sicker than she was last week."

Nicole nodded miserably. "Mrs. Redmond has been in the hospital since last Saturday night. At first Christy insisted that it was only temporary . . . but now . . . I'm not so sure."

I felt a tight knot in my chest, and for a moment I wasn't sure I was going to be able to breathe. I felt transplanted in time, back to when my own mother was lying in a hospital bed.

"I'm sorry, Nicole," I said, because there was really nothing else to say.

She rubbed her eyes, then gave me a baffled glance. "I don't understand—how did you know that Mrs. Redmond is sick? I never told you that."

"That's what I was going to tell you about," I told her. "The reason I wanted to meet Christy was that I recognized her from the hospital cancer ward.

I saw her in the waiting room there last year . . . when my own mom was dying from breast cancer."

Understanding began to dawn in Nicole's eyes. For a long time she didn't say anything. She simply sat there, looking sad and vulnerable and adorable in the lobster bib that now seemed absurdly out of place.

"Justin, I didn't know. I mean, you never mentioned your mom. . . . I figured you two didn't get along or something. I, uh, didn't want to pry."

"Sometimes talking about her is just too painful," I admitted. "She died last year, but often it feels more like last week."

"You wanted to talk to Christy about her mother?" Nicole asked. "That's why you wanted to meet her?"

I nodded. "At first I thought I wanted to talk to Christy just because I thought I might be able to offer her an empathetic ear." I paused, realizing that this was the most open, honest conversation I'd had with a girl since Laurie and I broke up. "But I finally realized that I need Christy's help too. I wanted to talk with someone about what it felt like to have a sick mother so that I could get some of my own feelings off my chest."

"I wish Christy would talk more to Jane and me," Nicole said, her voice contemplative. "It's like she believes that as long as she doesn't talk about her mom's illness, it won't be real."

"But you've been there for her," I stated. The fact wasn't even a question in my mind—I knew there was no way Nicole Gilmore would abandon a friend in need. "That's the important thing."

She nodded. "Jane and I have been at the hospital during every free moment. But Christy barely talks to us. . . . That's probably why she didn't tell me about your mom. She's sort of lost in her own world right now."

I knew how that felt, and my heart ached for Christy. But another part of my heart felt lighter than it had since my mother died. And that was because of Nicole.

"Do you want to go home?" I asked. "I'll understand if you're not in the mood to go to a dance."

"No way," Nicole proclaimed. "Christy found out that we were going to your prom tonight, and she practically made me sign a written contract saying I wouldn't back out on her account." She paused. "Now I understand at least part of why she felt so strongly. . . . Christy probably realizes that it's important for you to live your own life, now that there's nothing you can do for your mom."

And Christy was right. Just as Star had been. I glanced at my watch, shocked to see how much time had passed while Nicole and I had been talking.

"Nic, we've got a lot more to talk about tonight. But I think we better continue this conversation at the prom. It started half an hour ago."

As she stood to leave, I admired her all over again. Now that we had started this dialogue, I hoped I would succeed in convincing Nicole that she was the only "someone special" I wanted in my life. And if I was lucky . . . maybe tonight would end with a kiss rather than the supreme brush-off I received at our *last* prom. Anything was possible.

Twenty

Nicole

THE JEFFERSON HIGH prom committee had clearly outdone themselves. While the Union High prom had been a winter wonderland, this one was a Caribbean paradise. There were huge fake palm trees, thatched huts, tiny umbrellas in the punch, and sandboxes everywhere. Naturally everyone received a lei at the door.

"This is really something," I said to Justin. "You guys know how to throw a party."

Justin smiled and pointed toward the ceiling. "You'll notice that we too have the requisite disco ball."

"I'm impressed."

I felt my spirits lift as I watched dozens of couples approximating hula dances as the band played something that sounded vaguely Hawaiian. So what if Justin was just using me to get to some girl? He had become a good friend, and that was going to have to be enough.

Out of nowhere I felt a large hand clamp down on my shoulder. "So this is Nicole!" a deep voice announced. "We've never officially met, but Justin's been talking about you so much for the past week that I feel like we're already friends."

I turned around to find a guy with dark brown curly hair and warm hazel eyes grinning at me. A petite blond girl was standing beside him. "Uh . . ."

Justin stepped closer to me. "Nicole, this is my overly enthusiastic best friend, Sam. And this is his girlfriend, Maya."

"Hi. Nice to meet you," I greeted them. I was still reeling from the fact that Justin had been talking about me all week.

"Are you guys going to dance or *what?*" Sam asked. "Maya and I have already been out on the floor for almost an hour. I'm totally sweaty."

"Charming, isn't he?" Maya asked, her eyes sparkling. "But Sam is mine, and I love him."

I grinned at both Maya and Sam. They were exactly the kind of people I would have been friends with if I had gone to Jefferson High. If Justin and I were going out, I could imagine double dating with Sam and Maya every weekend. *Don't think like that,* I admonished myself. *It's not going to happen.*

So much had happened tonight that I was having a tough time remembering that tonight was just payback for last weekend. Justin and I had such a rapport. . . . It was as if we had known each other years, not days.

"If you guys don't mind, I think I'll follow Sam's advice and ask my date for a dance," Justin announced to his friends. He turned to me. "Nicole, will you do me the honor?"

I curtsied. "*Mais oui*, monsieur."

Justin took my hand and started to lead me toward the dance floor. It felt like déjà vu. But this time we weren't putting on a show for Rose and Madison. We were going to dance for the benefit of some nameless, faceless girl—who despite myself, I hated.

When we were a few steps away from Sam and Maya, Sam suddenly lunged forward and clasped my arm. "You're the best thing that's ever happened to Justin," he whispered. "I feel like I've finally got my best friend back."

I didn't know what to make of Sam's words as Justin and I continued toward the dance floor. Tonight was all about mixed signals . . . and I was more confused than ever.

"So where is she?" I asked as soon as we were on the dance floor. "Where is that special someone?"

I figured that if I said that phrase enough times, I would be able to accept the horrible fact that lay behind it. So far, it wasn't working.

The band struck up a slow tune, and Justin put his arms around me. His embrace was becoming tantalizingly familiar, and it was hard not to melt into him.

"Before I tell you about the 'special someone'

you keep mentioning, I want to finish the conversation we started at dinner," he told me softly.

"I'm not sure now is the time to talk about Christy's mom," I replied. I wasn't going to be able to keep it together if Justin and I allowed ourselves to think about Christy, at her mother's bedside at the hospital.

He shook his head. "This isn't about Mrs. Redmond—at least not directly," he told me. "It's sort of about my mom . . . but most of all, it's about me."

I nodded. Gazing into Justin's warm brown eyes, I probably would have agreed to talk about *anything*. And I was touched that he trusted me enough to discuss something that was obviously so painful. I wanted to be there for him—even if it was only as a friend.

"I used to have a girlfriend," Justin began. "Her name was—still is—Laurie, and I thought I was going to be in love with her for the rest of my life."

"Uh-huh . . ." Hearing a monologue about Justin's ex-girlfriend wasn't exactly what I had been expecting.

"When my mom got sick, Laurie bailed," Justin continued. "She couldn't deal with it. . . . She didn't *want* to deal with it."

"That's awful!" I exclaimed. I couldn't imagine leaving a friend—or a boyfriend—at a time like that.

He nodded. "It *was* awful. And my breakup with Laurie made my mother's death even harder than it already was. I felt totally isolated."

"You must have been so lonely. . . ." Thinking about Justin's grief made my eyes fill with tears. More than anything, I wished I had known him

176

then. I wished I could have been there for him during that horrible time.

"Somehow my mom's death and my breakup with Laurie got all mixed up in my head." His voice was quiet, but I could hear his words clearly, despite the band music. It was as if I was tuned in to Justin's thoughts as he spoke.

"I don't know what to say," I responded. "I can't imagine what that must have been like."

He smiled. "Don't be sad, Nic. I'm getting to the happy part of the tale." He paused. "Anyway, I convinced myself that if I swore off girls forever, I would never experience that pain again. I thought I could stay safe, living life like I was surrounded by an unbreakable bubble."

"But there's always pain," I said softly. "It's part of life."

"Exactly," Justin agreed. "But that's something I didn't realize—until this past week. I was shutting out pain—or so I thought—by not allowing myself to get close to another girl." He paused. "But I was also shutting out happiness."

"And now?" I asked.

He grinned. "And *now* I realize that I have to move on with my life. I'll always miss my mom, but that doesn't mean I should cut myself off from all that life has to offer."

"Is this where the 'special someone' comes in?" I asked. I hated to bring up the subject, but I couldn't help myself.

He nodded. "*You're* the special someone, Nicole.

You're the girl I was hoping to impress tonight."

"I . . . I . . ." I was speechless. And euphoric. And utterly turned upside down.

"Can I put one more condition on tonight?" he asked. "Just to make things even between us?"

"What is it . . . ?" I couldn't breathe.

"I want this to be a real date," he said softly, folding me even closer into his embrace.

I felt my entire body sort of light up. I would have thought I had misheard Justin, but there was no mistaking the heat in his gaze.

"I don't understand . . . ," I whispered. "Last week you didn't . . . I mean, Justin, you were so . . ." I couldn't find any words to express what I was trying to say.

"I wasn't interested in finding romance, Nicole," he said simply. "Like I said, I had sworn off girls for good." As he paused, I resisted the urge to fall deeper into his arms like a limp noodle. "Then I met you . . . and I can't ignore my feelings." He reached out and took my hand. "You're the girl of my dreams—only I didn't even know I was dreaming."

If the floor had opened up and swallowed me whole at that moment, I would have left the earth a happy girl. But the floor didn't open up. This was real. *It's just like a fairy tale after all. . . .*

For all of high school I had refused to compromise. I hadn't gone out with jerks on the football team just because they were considered the gods of Alta Vista. And I hadn't dated the nicer guys who made me yawn halfway through a conversation just so I would have something to do on Saturday night.

I had spent my time bonding with Jane and Christy, the two best friends a girl could have. And I had read books and listened to music, discovering who I was and who I wanted to be. There had been times when I was lonely, tempted to enter the mainstream of high-school life just so I could blend in with the crowd.

But I hadn't. And my patience had been worthwhile. The cocoon had slipped away, and I had emerged a butterfly, worthy of being the prom date of the greatest guy I had ever met.

"Nicole?" Justin's voice reached me through the haze of my whirling thoughts.

"What?" I asked, pinching myself on the arm—just to make sure.

"Is your answer yes? Will you agree that this is a *real* date . . . and will you agree to go on another one with me?"

"Yes!" I answered. "Yes!"

"There's one more thing I wanted to ask you," Justin said. We weren't even dancing now. We were just standing under the disco ball, staring into each other's eyes.

"What?" I asked again.

"This . . ." Justin held me in his arms, and I felt like I was defying gravity, floating on air.

For a long moment we looked at each other. Then he lowered his head . . . and kissed me. My heart melted as I felt his soft, firm lips against mine. I slid my arms around his neck, and the kiss deepened. The firecrackers I had experienced the times

179

Justin's fingers had grazed my bare skin were nothing compared to the sparks zipping through my veins now.

Until this moment I hadn't allowed myself to process just how intense my feelings for Justin had become. I had been too afraid of getting hurt to admit to myself just how much I wanted him to be a part of my life. Now . . . I felt more alive than I had during the past four years of high school.

At last Justin pulled away from me. "Thank you for finding me, Nicole," he said quietly. "You've changed my life."

Like I said before, I had never been the kind of girl who chased boys or dreamed about knights on white horses or wanted to wear a guy's picture in a locket around my neck. But all of that had changed the day that Justin Banks walked into Claire's Boutique with his little sister. Now I was a believer in long walks on the beach, candlelit dinners, and late-night study dates. I was a new woman—and I liked it.

"You've changed my life too," I whispered back.

And they lived happily ever after . . . , I thought, finishing the fairy tale that my life had become during the past few weeks.

Then I kissed Justin again . . . and realized that the *real* story was just beginning.

Do you ever wonder about falling in love? About members of the opposite sex? Do you need a little friendly advice but have no one to turn to? Well, that's where we come in . . . Jenny and Jake. Send us those questions you're dying to ask, and we'll give you the straight scoop on life and love.

DEAR JAKE

Q: *At the last school dance I spent most of the night dancing with a boy I know from one of my classes. We had a lot of fun, and I thought we hit it off really well. Well, Monday at school he acted like I had the plague. He wouldn't talk to me or even look at me in class. I have no idea what his problem is, but the whole thing is making me really uncomfortable. I'm starting to wonder if I imagined having fun with him at the dance or if I did something that completely turned him off. I'm totally clueless at this point. What do you think?*

JK, Oahu, HI

A: I doubt you did anything to turn him off. I suspect that he's got something weighing heavily on his mind, such as a girlfriend, or an exam, or maybe even problems at home. I'm not excusing his behavior—I just want to be sure that you don't take his behavior personally. Try asking him why he's avoiding you after such a great time at the dance. If he acts like he's never seen you before, be glad he's not talking to you! But maybe he'll open up.

Q: *I have a major crush on my brother's friend Jeff, who I know likes me too. Problem is, my brother has actually forbidden me to date his friends. Can you believe his nerve? He's also told his friends that I'm off-limits to* them. Jeff and I have talked about it, and we don't know what to do. We're not into sneaking around, but Jeff doesn't want to lose my brother's friendship—or get beat up! Do you think pursuing a relationship is worth it?

DT, Blakesburg, IA

A: Sounds to me like both you and Jeff need to have separate conversations with your brother. Jeff, from a friend's angle. And you, from a sister's angle. Your brother cannot control your life and tell you who you can or can't date. But your brother is allowed to feel uncomfortable about a buddy of his getting romantically involved with his sister. Talk it through and do what feels right to you in your heart.

DEAR JENNY

Q: *I went on a few dates with a guy friend of mine but realized I only like him as a buddy. When I told him how I felt, he got angry and started spreading rumors about me around school. I confronted him, and he actually had the nerve to tell me he'd take back everything he said if I agreed to be his girlfriend. I think he's a total jerk now, but I care about my rep. What should I do?*

AF, Salem, OR

A: Sometimes the best thing you can do is absolutely nothing at all. Any guy who spreads rumors about you is not worthy of your friendship, let alone your heart. And any guy who'd try to "blackmail" you into being his girlfriend isn't someone worthy of your time and energy. You were honest with him, and he reacted in the most immature way imaginable. Ignoring him—and rumors that'll fade fast anyway—is your best bet.

Q: *My boyfriend doesn't like my best friend—who happens to be a guy. Brian and I have been dating for about five months, but Anthony and I have known each other for years. Brian is jealous of the time I spend with Anthony, and he doesn't seem to get that we're only friends. I feel like I'm being pressured into choosing between the two of them, and it's starting to stress me out. Help!*

BL, Cleveland, OH

A: Sounds like you and your boyfriend could use a heart-to-heart talk about this. Ask him why he feels uncomfortable about your friendship with Anthony. Does Brian think you have romantic feelings for your friend? Does he worry you'll break up with him? Does he worry that Anthony will try to steal you away? Perhaps it's a matter of simply telling him he's got nothing to worry about. However, if he asks you to choose between him and your friend, then his jealousy might make your relationship impossible and not much fun.

Do you have any questions about love?
Although we can't respond individually to your letters,
you just might find your questions answered in our column.
Write to:
Jenny Burgess or Jake Korman
c/o 17th Street Productions, Inc.
33 West 17th Street
New York, NY 10011

Don't miss any of the books in *Love Stories*
—the romantic series from Bantam Books!